The Vatican Children

World of Shadows

Book II

By

Lincoln Cole

Published by Lincoln Cole, Columbus, 2017
Lincoln@LincolnCole.net
www.LincolnCole.net

Cover Design by M.N. Arzu
www.mnarzuauthor.com

Table of Contents

*"For if God spared not the angels
that sinned, but cast them down
to hell, and delivered them into
chains of darkness, to be reserved
to judgment;"*

- 2 Peter 2:4

Chapter 1

Outside, leaves and gravel crunched when a car pulled up to Arthur's cabin in the forests of Colorado. He'd expected it, so it didn't cause him any concern, and he didn't realize anything had gone amiss, in fact, until a second door slammed shut.

Alarmed, he jumped up from the couch he'd sat resting on and slid his gun off the coffee table. Then he made his way over to the window, careful to stay out of view. Had his hideout become compromised? He had anticipated that Father Niccolo Paladina would arrive just about now, but he had also expected for the priest to come alone.

His newly finished cabin sat deep in the middle of uninhabited forestry in Colorado, and it served as his sanctuary away from civilization. It would prove difficult to find even with a map and closely-detailed directions, which meant that either Niccolo had brought a friend with him—which would be bad—or someone else had just driven up.

Weapon held ready, he flipped the curtain aside and peeked out through the small gap.

Not his revolver sat in his hand, though, a fact which made him feel practically naked as he leaned against the wall. His revolver lay under the pillow in his bedroom. What he held was a tranquilizer gun designed to fire darts.

It didn't feel as heavy as his weapon of choice, the Colt revolver, which made it awkward in his hands. Also, it held only three darts and seemed cumbersome and tricky to load. He shifted it in his hand continually, willing it to become more comforting.

Arthur had opted to carry it, though, because he wanted to get used to using it. Some comfort lay in knowing his revolver waited nearby, along with a pair of shotguns and an assault rifle, but hopefully, he wouldn't need any of them.

When he saw the car sitting in front of his cabin, though, he relaxed and let out a sigh. In hindsight, he should have known: only one person would be brazen enough to bring a friend to his sanctuary uninvited.

"Frieda," he mumbled, sliding the tranquilizer gun away into his shoulder holster.

Frieda had just climbed out of the little blue sedan and now walked toward the cabin. She spoke to someone on the other side of the car, and it took a second for that person to walk around the hood and into his sightline.

Abigail.

"Uh oh." He groaned.

This was perfectly bad timing.

Arthur rushed over to the door of his cabin and out onto the front porch. Hastily, he closed the door behind him and used his body to block it.

"Hey, Frieda. Uh ... what's up?"

The woman stopped walking midstride, a suspicious frown blooming on her face.

"Hi, Arthur." She put out a hand to stop Abigail, and then turned her attention back to Arthur. "We've come here to visit."

"You didn't call ahead."

"I didn't think *we* had to," she said, nodding toward Abigail.

Abigail looked exhausted from the long drive, but she stood beaming at Arthur. The girl was closing in on her eighth birthday—by the best guesses of multiple physicians—and had long black hair and a narrow face.

He had to admit, just seeing her caused his heart to race and filled him with emotion. She represented his second chance at life, a chance to try again. This time, he would get it right.

She acted nothing like the little girl he had saved in the manor of West Virginia. Back then, those ten months ago, she had worn torn and tattered clothes and a vacant expression in her eyes, the broken shell of a little girl who had undergone years of torture and abuse.

Now, she just looked like a normal youngster.

Abigail seemed about to run up to hug him, but she

could sense the tension between him and Frieda. Instead, she kept glancing between them, a look of confusion on her young face.

"You don't have to call ahead," Arthur said. "I just expected someone else to show up, and you two caught me off-guard. What are you doing here?"

"We came to visit." Frieda folded her arms across her chest and gave him one of her famous looks of disapproval. "We've come out of our way, but it's been a few weeks since you checked in with us in person, and we wanted to make sure *you* were doing all right. What *are* you doing?"

The real question she asked was: *What are you hiding?* Arthur flashed her a look that he hoped conveyed they shouldn't discuss this in front of others. He didn't want to talk to her about it at all, but especially not in front of Abigail.

"As I said, I'm waiting for someone else to get here."

"Who? That priest you met in Everett? Did the Vatican clear him to work with you?"

He hesitated. "Yes, but not exactly."

"What do you mean?"

"He didn't ask for clearance from the Vatican. Not yet, at least."

Arthur ignored the look of shock on Frieda's face. He strode down the front steps of his cabin and wrapped Abigail in a hug. Then he lifted her up in the air and swung her around.

"Abi," he said. "It's so great to see you!"

She hugged him back and giggled as he spun her. "I missed you!" she said.

"Me too."

He looked over Abigail's shoulder at Frieda. She seemed about to say something else, so he mouthed, *Not a good time.*

Frieda held up her hands in question and raised her eyebrows, but she didn't say anything. Gently, Arthur set Abigail back onto the leaves and dirt. He knelt in front of her so that they came eye-to-eye.

"Been stuck in the car for a long time, huh?"

"Yep," she said. "It was *so* boring."

With a grin, he glanced at Frieda, and then leaned closer to Abigail to whisper conspiratorially, "I know what you mean. Did she just listen to her classical music?"

Abigail giggled and whispered, "The *whole* way."

He laughed. "Do you want to go play?"

She nodded. "Uh huh."

"I think I have a soccer ball out behind the cabin. Not a lot of room to run around in the woods, but it's better than nothing. If you want to go find it, I'll come right out, and we can kick it around some."

"Okay."

When she headed for the front door of the cabin, he caught her arm and pointed to the west. "Not that way. Head around the side."

Abigail nodded and then took off running in the direction he had pointed. He didn't have a soccer ball out there just now—it sat in one of the closets inside the cabin—but he figured searching for it would keep Abigail busy for at least a few minutes.

Once she went out of earshot, he turned to face Frieda and her withering expression of annoyance. She still had her arms folded across her chest, and if looks could kill ...

"What did you do?"

"Why would you assume that I *did* something?" he said as innocently as he could.

Her silence spoke volumes. Awkward, he stared at her, and finally, she let out an exaggerated sigh and rubbed her forehead.

"Arthur. How long have we known each other?"

"A *long* time. Too long, you might say."

"Exactly. Now, will you tell me what you have hidden from me in your cabin, or do I have to tear the place down and find out for myself?"

"It isn't a big deal."

"I'll be the judge of that. You went behind my back already and invited that priest to work with you."

"He invited himself."

"Mmhmm."

"Like I said, it isn't that big a deal. Promise you won't overreact?"

"Arthur, if you don't get out of my way and let me inside, I'll shoot you."

She meant it as a joke, of course.

At least, he felt pretty sure she did.

Still, he stepped aside and gestured for her to pass. "After you."

Frieda walked up the steps to the cabin door, but not without a slight hesitation in her gait. Her right hand rested against her hip, close to her concealed pistol.

She reached out and grabbed the door handle, but didn't turn it.

"I'm not about to find a dead body in there, am I?"

"'Dead' is such a strong word ..."

She turned and glowered at him.

"Kidding," he said, padding his hands in the air to calm her. "Just joking. She's still alive."

"She?"

Arthur didn't reply. Frieda stared at him a moment longer before turning back toward the entryway. Gently, she turned the handle and pushed open the front door.

Inside lay a small foyer with coat racks and hooks on the opposite wall. It led off to a kitchen on the right and living room on the left. Inside the living room sat a maroon love seat and armchair combo, a cumbersome hardwood coffee table that Arthur had built himself, and a fireplace that roared with a pile of burning logs.

Next to the fireplace sat a blonde woman in her mid-to-late forties with greenish eyes. He had tied her to a chair with duct tape around her wrists and ankles and another strip across her mouth to keep her from shouting. Her hair had matted, and she had raccoon eyes from wearing her makeup for too long.

When Frieda walked into the cabin, her eyes went wide, and she thrashed the chair around frantically. She made moaning noises into the tape, hoping to get her attention.

However, when Arthur followed Frieda into the room, she stopped struggling and narrowed her eyes. The woman glanced between the two. Upon realizing that they had come in here together, her expression shifted from hope to fear, and she attempted to cower lower into her seat.

Frieda stayed silent for a long moment, just staring at the woman, before she wheeled around to face Arthur. "You've got to be kidding me."

"It looks worse than it is."

"It *looks* like you kidnapped this woman."

Arthur hesitated. "Okay, so maybe it is exactly what it looks like. But, the thing is, this setup was more for *effect* than anything else. I've kept her in the basement for the last day or so, but I only brought her up here a short while ago."

"Why?"

"I've waited for Father Paladina, and I wanted to get *his* reaction to seeing her like this. Not yours, and *certainly* not Abigail's."

"I thought you'd done hurting people?" she said, with just a hint of mockery in her voice.

"I'm done killing people," he said. "But that isn't what this is about. What I do ... what *we* do is dangerous and ugly, and if I'm to work with Niccolo—a freaking priest—then I need him to understand that things won't be easy or good."

Frieda corrected, "What we do is what we are *told* to do. How the hell can you work with this priest without the Vatican's consent? Or, did you forget that we're in hot water right now?"

"We can't wait for all of this to go through the proper channels. It will take too long, and whatever the bishop has planned is happening *now*. Leopold Glasser needs to be stopped."

"You aren't even officially assigned to this case, yet."

"A formality," Arthur said. "Since *you* will assign me."

"I will?"

"You run the Hunters. Just tell the Council I'll be busy solving this crisis for a while."

"That's all well and good, but what about Niccolo? I can't assign him to this case."

"The assignment won't matter. Niccolo works as an exorcist. He has the Church's backing and a lot of slack in what cases he decides to pursue."

"Enough slack to hang himself, you mean. Are you sure you want to get strung up next to him? The Vatican continues to investigate everything, and our funding has depleted. If this goes sideways ... well, then I can't help you."

"I wouldn't expect you to anyway. All I know is that *this* needs to get taken care of, and if we wait for a few weeks for the Church to catch up, then it'll be too late."

"You hope the ends will justify the means."

"I know they will," Arthur said. Then he shrugged. "Seventy percent. What I do know is that this needs to get investigated, and I also know that Niccolo can't do this alone. Neither can I."

A look of surprise flashed across her face. "I never expected those words to come out of your mouth."

"I told you, I'm turning over a new leaf. This is the new and improved Arthur."

"Sounds more like you dug up the entire tree," she said. She studied him for a second, tapping her chin. "Fine, I'll back your play and do my best to get the Vatican on board with this, but you need to take more care about things like *this*. No more kidnapping."

"I told you, it's just for effect to get a rise out of the priest."

"What if Abigail had seen this?"

"I didn't know you planned on coming. You could have called."

"I didn't think you would have a prisoner in your living room."

"How long have we known each other?" he asked.

She smiled, brushing a spot of dust off the sleeve of her impeccably clean white shirt. "Touché."

The tension passed, and Frieda relaxed. They had known each other for many years, ever since Arthur had begun his training as a Hunter. She wouldn't stay mad at him for long, and it came as a relief to know that she had his back. He had stepped out pretty far onto a branch with this case, and he liked having a safety net in case it broke.

"Do you want something to drink?" he asked. "I have a few things in the fridge. Maybe even a bottle of champagne."

"Champagne?"

"I think you gave it to me when I started building this place. I didn't want to drink it until I finished."

"That was, like, ten years ago."

He shrugged. "Just means it's well aged."

"Water is fine. I'll bring something out to Abigail, too," Frieda said. "I'm sure she's thirsty after the drive."

"I have some juice."

"Is that well-aged, too?"

"No. Just bought it yesterday. Apple juice."

Frieda half-smiled at him. "You and your apple juice. Do you drink anything else?"

"It's cheap."

Frieda glanced over at the woman tied to the chair. "Who is she?"

"Desiree Portman," Arthur said. "She sent that correspondence to the bishop I told you about a couple of days ago. The letters went back years."

"A friend?"

"I thought so, at first. Now, I'm not so sure."

Frieda glanced at him. "What do you mean?"

Arthur turned and walked into the kitchen, making sure they stood out of Desiree's earshot, and Frieda followed. "The correspondence is friendly, in general, but what she writes holds an undercurrent of fear. I don't have *his* letters, only hers, but she seems to exaggerate her compliments and never has an ill word about anything."

"So, you think he coerced her?"

"I believe she's one of his victims," Arthur said. "Too afraid to come forward and speak out against him, so she goes along with whatever he wants. I think the bishop abused her."

"Physically?"

"Don't know, but definitely mentally. I've dug into her past, but so far, haven't come up with much beyond broad details."

"How did they know each other?"

"She went to a Catholic School as a young woman, and he was the resident priest."

"You think he leveraged his power over her?"

"I'm sure he did."

"Then why would you kidnap her? You think she knows something?"

"I reckon they talked a *lot*, and whether or not she knows something is inconsequential. He kept close tabs on her, judging by the letters. And he's bound to have messed up and said something we can use to track him down or find out what he's after."

"That's a big leap. You called her a victim. Why would he tell her anything?"

"A slip," Arthur said. "She might have kept his letters. Besides, I didn't have a lot of other options. My best guess is that he still keeps an eye on her. Her going missing like this is bound to bring him out of hiding if he thinks we can use her against him."

"Maybe," Frieda said, though she didn't sound too convinced.

The truth was, Arthur didn't feel that convinced himself. Kidnapping Desiree came down to a spur-of-the-moment decision based on the fact that he had almost nothing else to go by. The bishop had disappeared without a trace when he left Everett, and none of Arthur's contacts had any idea where he might have gone.

His hope where Niccolo was concerned came two-fold: first, he could use Desiree to test Niccolo and find out how sincere he was in trusting Arthur. Niccolo had proclaimed himself willing to do *anything* to catch Bishop Glasser. And Arthur wanted to see how true that commitment would prove when things got messy.

Secondly, however, he *did* have a hope that Desiree might know something they could use against Leopold. He hadn't managed to get much out of her in the last twenty-four hours, but Niccolo was an easy man to trust. Arthur hoped that she might open up to Niccolo about whatever relationship she'd had with the bishop.

Though a long shot, they didn't have anything to lose. If nothing else, it would keep them occupied while they waited for news.

"I guess Abigail will want to come inside by now," Frieda said, interrupting him from his thoughts.

"I know," he said. Then he pulled a bottle of apple juice out of the fridge and poured a cup for Abigail and another for Frieda. He handed them to her. "Give me two minutes to get everything cleaned up and Desiree back into the basement."

Frieda nodded and headed out the back door of the cabin. He watched her go and then let out a long sigh.

He hadn't expected those two to show up, but it gladdened him they had. They threw a wrench into his plans, but it still gave a bright spot to his day. He'd stayed here alone with his prisoner for the last twenty-four hours, and it had worn on him.

He poured another glass of apple juice, and then went back into the living room and over to the woman he had tied to the chair. She looked terrified of him, and rightly so, but he had no intention of harming her at all.

In fact, Arthur would have taken her back home when he found out she didn't have any solid information. She might have managed to identify him, but he doubted she would. The problem now was that he worried about her safety. He wouldn't have any choice but to keep her here until they had dealt with the bishop.

Gently, he cut the duct tape loose except for the strip covering her mouth. This one, he peeled the edge loose, and then before she could stop him, he ripped it off.

She let out a small squeal when he did it, and he could only shrug in response. "Sorry. It's worse if I try to do it slowly."

The woman didn't respond. He offered her the cup of apple juice, but she didn't take it. She hadn't eaten much since he'd first kidnapped her, which didn't surprise him.

He led her over to the basement door, unlocked it, and then guided her with care down the stairs.

His prison, as Frieda liked to call it, consisted of a few enclosed rooms that he'd custom built using metal bars and cement. Dim, it had only one small window in the corner. Although it had an overhead light, it did little to make the place feel any more welcoming than a dungeon.

Desiree barely struggled, terrified, and he felt more than a little bad for what he'd done to her in all of this. He had believed that she might be an unwilling participant in her and the bishop's relationship, but after spending the last few days with her, Arthur had become sure that she was the bishop's victim before as much as Arthur's now.

Ideally, she would have proven to have involvement in protecting and hiding the bishop. He'd hoped that she was someone he confided in and that she would give up the man's location, but it proved no use. An innocent bystander, she turned out completely useless to his current mission.

When he guided her over and locked her back into her cell, she sobbed.

"I'm sorry for this," he said. "Probably, you don't believe me, but I really am."

"Please, let me go," she murmured, lips quivering. The poor woman wouldn't even look him in the eyes.

"I would, but then you wouldn't be safe."

"I'm not safe *here*."

She had no idea how wrong she was. Knew nothing of the supernatural world around them and that she had now become connected to it. The problem was, she only thought of the bishop as terrifying to *her*. He'd victimized and mistreated her for years, but she had *no idea* how horrible the man could actually be. She lacked the imagination to understand what might happen to her if the bishop thought her a threat to his survival.

"I truly am sorry," he said. "Maybe one day you will understand and forgive me."

He closed the cell, locked it, and then walked over to the stairs. He paused, though, before heading up and glanced back at her.

"If not, though, that's okay too."

Then he headed back up to the main floor of his cabin.

✳✳✳

By the time he made it up the stairs, Frieda had gone back inside, though she didn't have Abigail with her. She leaned against the counter and watched through a window that looked behind the cabin. When the basement door opened, she glanced over but soon returned her gaze.

"She didn't want to come inside," Frieda said. "She's too busy chasing butterflies."

"We have butterflies outside?"

She shrugged. "Who knew?"

Arthur walked over to the window next to her, and she nodded out toward the forested area surrounding them. Abigail played out in the trees, dancing around and laughing.

"What happened to playing soccer?"

"That's old news," Frieda said. Her tone sounded playful ... at least, as playful as her tone ever became. She took a sip of her apple juice and then looked at it with distaste. "You find one of the cheapest juices the world has to offer, and then buy the cheapest bottle of it. I'll never understand you.”

“Maybe you should pay me more.”

“I don’t pay you anything.”

“See? My point exactly.”

“I prefer orange juice.”

“I don’t have ‘orange juice’ money right now.”

“We might be broke, but we can still afford a few luxuries.”

Arthur laughed. “It’s been hell for you, hasn’t it? No more private jets and expensive hotel rooms.”

“I’ll make do.”

“I’m sure you will.”

He looked back out the window. Just watching Abigail play in the trees filled him with a peace and tranquility he hadn’t experienced in a long time. He could hardly believe she could have become so happy and free, considering everything that had happened to her. She had changed so much since living under the control of the cult.

When he had found her out in the manor in West Virginia, strapped down to the table, she had looked terrified and fragile. It felt nice to see her like this: a bright spot in his normally dark life, like a ray of sunshine piercing through a cloudy sky.

“You should let her go.”

It took Arthur a moment to realize that Abigail meant the woman in the basement and not Abigail. Even then, the words unsettled him. He had tried to adopt Abigail for months, and even though a large part of him worried that they would say no, another small part had grown terrified that they would say yes.

“I would let Desiree go if I could,” he said.

“People will look for her.”

“She lives alone,” Arthur said. “No family. No friends to speak of. We crossed four state lines, and no one’s reported her missing yet.”

“Still. You made a rash decision.”

“I know,” Arthur said. “But I can’t *unmake* it.”

"You will tip off the bishop that you've gone after him."

"That's the point. He knows we're after him already. With luck, this will cause him to start panicking and make a mistake."

"What if he doesn't?"

"Then, we'll still find him," Arthur said, unconvincingly.

Frieda changed the topic, "Niccolo sounds like he could prove useful. You said Niccolo exorcised a demon in Everett?"

Arthur nodded. "His first. The first he'd ever faced, actually, alone or otherwise."

"No small feat."

"He *can* be useful." Arthur nodded. "But if he'll get in my way or cause problems, then I need to know that sooner rather than later."

"It's good to see you working with someone else, but we need to stay open and honest with the Church about all of this. I don't like misleading them."

"We will," Arthur said. "We shall tell them everything as soon as we capture Glasser and can turn him over to them."

"You think he has someone working for him inside the Church?"

"He has to. Probably a few people. No way has he gotten where he has by doing this alone. I promise, Frieda, that we will report everything to the Vatican as soon as we have something concrete to report."

Frieda hesitated. "So, here we are: untrusted by the Church, broken and without funding, and now we plan to withhold information from them about a bishop that has treated with demons. Do I have it about right?"

Arthur smiled over at her. "What could possibly go wrong?"

She didn't answer, but he could feel the worry emanating from her. Any other Hunter in her organization, he knew, and she would have flatly refused all of his demands. He didn't like disabusing her trust, but he also didn't plan to fail in capturing the bishop. All he needed was a little bit of time.

"The Council plans to vote real soon," Frieda said, suddenly. She didn't explain what she meant, but she didn't have to either.

The vote that she spoke of would decide whether or not Arthur would be allowed to adopt Abigail as his lawful daughter.

The issue about whether or not they would have her executed had closed weeks earlier, thank God, but this issue hadn't turned out any easier for them to resolve.

Abigail not having any paperwork caused a problem. It meant that they couldn't find out who she was before the cult had kidnapped her. All they knew was the little girl they rescued from the cult, and she didn't remember anything.

They worked to track down her past, but the Ninth Circle had done a meticulous job of scrubbing her identity from the world. They didn't yet know where Abigail came from, how long the cult had held her prisoner, or who her family was or if she should be returned to them.

The first and preferable option would be to return her to her rightful family, and that felt perfectly all right with Arthur. But, after over ten months of searching, they still didn't even know where to begin looking.

As such, Arthur had offered to take her in and raise her. The problem of his adopting her stemmed from the fact that few members of the Council trusted him.

After the stunt he had pulled in West Virginia and all the people he'd killed, he doubted they ever would again. He had become dangerous, a loose cannon, and he could appreciate their concern.

To be honest, he wouldn't have trusted himself either. Not after what he had done, and no matter how many times he told the Council that he had changed and had become a new man, they didn't believe it.

He couldn't feel sure if he did, either.

Hopefully, their decision would give an affirmative, and

he would become the little girl's rightful guardian, but it wasn't his choice to make. Up to this point, Abigail had lived with Frieda in Germany.

Arthur hoped he could take her with him in the near future and look after her. He had spent a lot of time visiting with her these last few months and found her to be a sweet and brilliant young girl.

As for the actual vote …

Frieda wouldn't admit it to him, but she had put off calling for a vote from the Council because of worried motivations. If she put the question of Abigail's guardianship before the Council turned down the idea of Arthur adopting her, then the odds of being able to bring it up again would significantly reduce. Frieda wanted to make sure that when she presented the idea of Arthur adopting Abigail, it would pass for definite.

It encouraged Arthur to think that she might have enough votes to make it a reality.

"When?"

"I don't know, exactly," she said. "Schedules conflict, and we rarely meet in person or over the phone. Jun still feels pissed with you, too, and I've had to do a lot of smoothing over."

"I won't apologize for what I did."

"I wouldn't ask you to. Nor would Jun. But, there was probably a better way to handle it."

Arthur hesitated, and then conceded, "Maybe."

"In any case, it will happen soon. It could take two weeks or two months."

"Okay. That'll give me enough time to track down the bishop and get my affairs in order," he said. "She's traveled with you?"

"Yes. It's seemed rather hectic. I've moved around to do some damage control. With our funding cut, I've spent a lot of time re-evaluating our investments and consolidating our assets."

"Has she behaved herself?"

"She's made an excellent travel companion. Though, I'm not sure she would say the same about me."

"Just your music."

Frieda scoffed, "Whatever she might say, she loves Tchaikovsky. You do, too, if I recall?"

"Only when I travel with you."

Frieda laughed. "I'll feel sorry to see her go."

Arthur nodded, but Frieda was simply being polite for Arthur's sake. A loner, she kept to herself mostly, and taking care of a young and rambunctious child brought more than a mild annoyance for her.

She would never admit as much aloud, but Arthur knew she only tolerated Abigail because of him.

Like most such things, he wasn't quite certain how that made him feel.

"Will you take her home?" Frieda asked.

The question caught Arthur off-guard. He knew exactly which home she meant, and it wasn't this one. Just thinking about it sent waves of hurt and sorrow through his body. He ached with loss.

"No," he said, finally. "I won't return there. That isn't my home any longer."

He hadn't gone to his farmhouse in Ohio since the cult had murdered his family. He wouldn't even set foot there and didn't know if he ever wanted to return. Arthur had tried on multiple occasions, but each time, he found himself unable to finish the drive up the dirt road to his old house.

To be honest, he barely even thought about the place anymore. Now, it had become a distant memory full of heartache and loss.

Another life.

"Here, then? Will you guys live here?"

"Maybe."

"You need to go back there," Frieda said. "If only to find closure and move on."

"I can't," he said. "I should just sell the place as is."

"No," she said, forcefully. Her sharp tone surprised

him. "Not until you go back at least once."

Arthur hesitated. In all honesty, he had no intention of ever selling the old farmhouse. It had remained in his family for many generations, and the thought of parting with it seemed unfathomable. However, he also had no intention of going back in the near future. He just wanted to forget about it.

"Fine," he said, if only to get her to drop the subject. "I won't sell the place, but I also won't go back. Not yet, at least."

"Good," she said, glancing down at her watch. "We need to get going. We have a long drive ahead of us, and this took us quite far out of our way. Abigail just missed you and wanted to see you."

Arthur nodded. He would have asked for them to stay, at least for a day or two, but he expected Father Paladina to arrive at any moment and needed to get back to work.

"Let me say my goodbyes."

"Of course. It will give me a chance to finish drinking my terrible juice."

He chuckled and headed outside. He found Abigail dancing in the trees about two-hundred feet away from the cabin. She had a bright smile on her face and barely noticed him striding toward her.

She had painful memories from her time with the cult, though they became less and less powerful as time passed. The more separation she had from her tribulations with the cult, the better things got for her, but he doubted the memories would ever go away completely. The trauma she had faced ...

... he could hardly believe she could still get out of bed in the mornings.

A tough little lass, for sure.

"Hey, kiddo," he said, stopping a few feet from her. She glanced up at him. "It's time for you and Frieda to get back on the road."

Abigail frowned. "Already? Can't we stay a bit longer?

We can leave tomorrow."

"Sorry, but no can do," he said. "Don't worry, though; we'll get to spend a lot of time together in the near future."

"You promise?"

"I promise."

"Okay."

She didn't sound like she believed him fully, but she didn't argue any further either. Without a word, she walked over, took his hand, and they walked back toward the cabin.

"Have you been going to school?"

She shook her head. "Frieda has taught me stuff. She says we move around too much to enroll me anywhere."

"Oh? What have you learned?"

"Things."

"What kinds of things?"

She shrugged. "Math, reading, a little bit of history. That kind of stuff."

"That's good," he said.

It surprised Arthur to learn that Frieda had homeschooled her, but it made sense, as putting her in a normal school wouldn't be good for anyone, and with Frieda needing to stay on the move constantly, it became important that Abigail stayed ready to leave at a moment's notice.

Plus, Frieda was an incredibly intelligent and well-educated woman, and he had no doubt that Abigail received a high-quality education.

They made it back to the cabin. Frieda stood waiting out front, resting against her car and just watching them. She had a pair of sunglasses on now, even though it stayed relatively shady in the forest.

"Ready to go, Abi?" she called as they walked up. "We still have a long way to go to get to our hotel for the night."

"Why can't we just stay here?"

"You can later," Arthur said. "Right now, it's too busy, though."

Abigail frowned. "Okay."

Then she hugged Arthur and raced over to the car,

sliding into the passenger seat with a frown. Frieda gave Arthur one last look—full of sadness and disapproval—before climbing into the driver's seat and turning on the car.

After a few moments, they headed back down the dirt road and away from the cabin. Arthur watched them go and thought about what Frieda had told him about the vote. He might become Abigail's lawful guardian soon.

On the one hand, that thrilled him. On the other, though ...

He felt terrified.

Already, he had lost one family. So had she. The thought of building another one with her and then losing her, too, stopped him cold.

Maybe he should tell Frieda to drop the issue with the Council. They could put her into foster care or up for adoption in any number of states or countries. Perhaps he could find another family to keep her safe and let her grow up as a normal little girl.

After all, would she ever find safety or peace with him?

Just seeing Abigail made him feel a lot better, like a weight had lifted from his shoulders. And seeing her smiling and happy made him think that maybe, just maybe, good did exist in the world. Perhaps it wasn't all evil.

Evil, Arthur thought, *like Bishop Glasser*.

He reminded himself that he had work to do and pushed the errant thought from his mind. Then he turned back to the cabin where he had the woman locked in his basement. She provided his only good lead to find out where the bishop hid, and he would need to get through to her if he were to bring the man to justice.

Chapter 2

By the time Niccolo made it to Arthur's cabin in the woods of Colorado, he'd grown tired, frustrated, and annoyed. He had first turned onto the dirt road leading into the forest early in the morning, and now the sky grew ever darker.

He also felt immensely hungry and wanted nothing more than to get some hot food into his belly. He hadn't thought to bring any victuals or water with him on the drive, and hadn't even imagined that he might need it.

As he drove up, he saw Arthur sitting on the porch in a rocking chair, and if anything, Arthur looked even more frustrated and annoyed than him. The man stood and walked down the stairs of the porch while Niccolo parked.

"You're late," Arthur said as soon as Niccolo climbed out of his car.

"I know."

"Like, very late. A lot later than I anticipated. I had honestly begun to think you had changed your mind and wouldn't come at all."

"Do you know how difficult this place was to find?"

"That's the point," Arthur said. "If my cabin proved easy to find, then people would *find* it. I figured you would get here, though, because I gave you explicit instructions."

"Terrible instructions. I missed the same turn three times," Niccolo said, dryly. "I didn't realize the 'giant cottonwood tree' you used as a marker had been cut down. I kept backtracking and driving past the turn."

Arthur shrugged, and then stretched. He walked back up the steps and over to the door. "I'll just have to remember not to let you navigate if we have to go anywhere."

Niccolo decided to ignore the jab, at least until he had eaten a good meal. Right now, he felt too hungry to care much about what Arthur said. Instead, he followed him into the cabin.

It looked quite a bit bigger than he had expected or seemed on the outside. A fire blazed in the living room off to the left, and the warm air felt great on his skin. Even better, the smell of cooked food wafted through the entire place.

"Dinner is ready," Arthur said, heading to the right into what appeared like a kitchen. "I figured you would feel hungry when you got here."

"Starving."

"I hope you like canned beans and Vienna sausages."

"I hate both," Niccolo said, "but, right now, I'm hungry enough that I don't care."

Arthur chuckled and led him over to where the food cooked. A gas stove had a pan simmering atop it, and he scooped them each out a bowl. Niccolo accepted it graciously and then followed him back into the living room to eat. It had only a huge coffee table about knee height, so he held the plate on his lap as he ate.

The only sound for the next couple of minutes came from them eating. The stew had sat simmering for a long time, and it tasted well seasoned. Niccolo, honestly, couldn't tell if the food was good or if he just felt that hungry.

Finally, he set his bowl on the coffee table and leaned back on the couch. Arthur followed suit a few bites later.

"Want more?"

"Not just now. Maybe in a bit."

"No problem. We don't have a lot of options, but we do have a lot of stuff."

"Canned goods?"

"Mostly. It gets tough bringing anything else out here with the long drive."

"Did you build this place?"

"Yeah. Took several years, and I only finished it recently."

"No one else knows about it?"

"Nope. Wouldn't be that well hidden if a lot of people knew it existed. Frieda and a few Hunters know, but that's it."

"It looks quite impressive."

"The government owns the land, and it lies buried

inside state and national forests. Only a handful of access roads even come out this direction, and none of them pleasant to drive on. It provides my haven out here in the middle of nowhere."

"You built it by hand? Did you have any help?"

"My brother, mostly."

"Brother?"

"Yeah, he lives in Ohio. I started the foundations a long time ago but never had the time to work on a consistent basis. I would just pick at it now and again, expanding constantly. Then, after my wife and daughter got murdered, I just settled down and finished it. I didn't want to move back into my family's home. It brought a constant reminder of what happened."

Niccolo nodded. "Of course."

"So, more or less, I've lived here or on the road for the last several months. Finished building the place not long before I went to Everett, actually. Rough, since I'm always on the move."

"Rarely have I traveled, myself. Not an enviable lifestyle," Niccolo said. "I've always had a sort of desire to become a world traveler. A wanderlust. But, now, I just wish I were back home in the comforts of my apartment."

"I hope you haven't grown homesick already," Arthur said. "Because we're just getting started."

✳✳✳

After cleaning up the remains of their lukewarm and unpleasant dinner, Arthur showed Niccolo to a small bedroom in the back of the cabin where he could unload his bags and rest. It looked like a multi-purpose room converted recently into sleeping quarters with only a lumpy twin mattress and spotted covers on the floor for him.

On the short tour that Arthur gave him, he had a chance to see the cabin's food stores, and didn't feel at all impressed. It looked like he would have to suffer many more terrible meals of canned and processed food in the future.

Then, before Niccolo could ask any more questions, Arthur disappeared into the basement of the cabin. He didn't offer an explanation or ask for Niccolo to follow him. In fact, he didn't seem to want him to come along. In confusion, Niccolo just watched him go.

Not that he cared overly much right now, anyway. Exhausted, he needed a break after the long drive. He headed back out to his rental car to gather up his belongings and brought them back to his room.

Unlike his previous trip to Everett, Washington, this time, he came completely prepared for any paranormal situation that might arise. Anything that could involve his duties as an Exorcist. He had a Stole, a new rosary he'd commissioned from the local craftsman who'd crafted his previous one, and all the crosses, Bibles, and religious symbols he could get his hands on at short notice.

His bag seemed to weigh a few hundred pounds when he hefted it back to his room. He didn't know what he would need or what situations he might face in this misadventure, but with Arthur around, anything remained possible.

Once he got back to the room, he laid down for a while. The lumpy bed smelled like sawdust, but he considered it only a minor nuisance considering how tired he'd grown.

He planned to lay down for just a minute to clear his head. The next item on his agenda was to find Arthur and ask about their plans, but he found himself dozing off before the opportunity arose.

The sound of a door slamming somewhere outside of his room awakened him a short while later. It jolted him into alertness, and he sat groggily in the darkness for a full minute before he got his bearings. The sunlight had gone, and he could see barely even a few inches in front of his face.

Niccolo dragged himself to his feet, he couldn't have slept for more than a few hours, but he felt significantly worse than when he'd laid down.

He found Arthur out in the living room waiting for him.

He leaned against the wall with his arms folded, watching Niccolo approach with a bemused expression on his face.

"A pleasant nap?"

Niccolo only moaned in response. "Where will I find your restroom?"

"The outhouse is out back." Arthur gestured toward the door at the rear of the house. He held the pose for a moment, watching Niccolo with a half-smile on his face, before continuing, "But, since the generator is running, it's down the hall behind you."

"You have running water?"

"Very clean at that. I didn't find it easy drilling for the pump, but it's some of the freshest water you'll ever taste."

Niccolo didn't want to admit how glad he felt that he wouldn't need to step out into the uninviting forest to relieve himself. He turned and headed into the facilities, splashing water on his face and slapping his cheeks. Arthur had told the truth. The water felt cold and clean and quite excellent.

When he made it back to the living room, he felt more awake and much better. The food had settled his stomach, and the nap had rejuvenated him. Arthur stood heating water on the stove and glanced over at him when he approached.

"Tea or coffee?"

"Instant coffee?"

"Mmhmm."

"Tea, then. Earl Grey if you have it."

Arthur didn't reply, but a moment later, he handed Niccolo a small platter with a steaming cup of water and a tea bag. No label, and for definite, it didn't smell like Earl Grey. Arthur nodded toward a bag of sugar on the corner of the counter but made no move toward it himself.

Niccolo dipped the bag into the water for a moment, watching the inky liquid spread. Arthur, he noticed, poured himself a cup of coffee and then mixed in equal parts cream and sugar.

They stood in silence for a moment, relaxing and

sipping their beverages. Finally, Arthur turned to face Niccolo and set his cup on the counter beside him.

"Not too comfortable out here, are you?"

"Of course not," Niccolo said. "You are?"

"I enjoy the quiet. It's more peaceful than you might imagine, though it does get cold at night."

"Cold?"

"No central heat. We only have a fireplace in the living room for heat but nothing in the bedrooms except blankets. Certainly, no central air. I run the generator when I need it. The gas powers the stoves."

"Ah, that explains the flannel blankets," Niccolo said. "Here I thought you simply wanted to make me itchy."

A look of surprise flashed across Arthur's face. "A joke?"

"I've been known to make a few from time-to-time."

"I thought the Vatican prohibited it."

Niccolo sipped his tea. "Only when I'm *at* the Vatican."

"You hungry?"

Niccolo still felt famished, but the thought of eating more canned goods turned his stomach. "Not right now."

"You'll get used to the food," Arthur said, noting the expression on his face. "After a while, you won't even notice how bad it tastes."

"I'm not sure I want to."

Arthur shrugged. "Don't worry; we won't be here too long. At least, that's the hope."

"Oh? Do we have a lead?"

"Not yet, but I do have quite a few people considering it. Something is bound to turn up."

"What about the woman that Bishop Glasser spoke of in his letters? Desiree something."

"Desiree Portman."

"Yes. What about her? Have you considered talking to her about the bishop?"

"Yes. And no," Arthur said. "I spoke to her, but she turned out a dead end."

Niccolo nearly spat out his tea. "What do you mean

did?"

"Don't worry; I didn't hurt her. I spoke to her at length and feel confident she doesn't know where the bishop has hidden."

"You spoke to her? When?"

"This morning," Arthur said, without missing a beat. "I have her in the basement."

Niccolo's jaw hung open. Fear mounted in the pit of his stomach. "She's what?"

"In the basement." Arthur sipped his tea. "Rather unhappily, I might add."

Niccolo's hands trembled, and he set the tea down on the counter. "Arthur ... what did you do?"

"Nothing *we* can't undo," Arthur said. "At least, mostly. I haven't harmed her, only questioned her."

"Here?"

"It seemed the best place."

"With her consent?"

Arthur shrugged. "I didn't ask."

Niccolo's voice rose in pitch and timbre, "You mean you kidnapped her?"

"That's one way of looking at it."

"You can't just *kidnap* people," Niccolo shouted, shaking his head in disbelief.

He rubbed his face while his mind attempted to process what Arthur had told him. The man had kidnapped a woman and brought her *here,* and that made Niccolo an accessory to his crime.

"You know, kidnapping people isn't that hard," Arthur said. "As long as no one sees you take them, and you get them over state lines in a hurry, it's not that difficult at all."

"I don't mean *you* can't. I mean you *can't.*"

"I can, and I will, when necessary," Arthur said. Even while Niccolo raised his voice, Arthur's remained calm and even. "Don't worry; she remains perfectly safe and well taken care of. I wouldn't dream of hurting her, and I intend to return her home as soon as we have this ordeal over with."

Niccolo shook his head and walked toward the door to the basement. He needed to fix this problem ... somehow ... before it got out of hand.

"That isn't the point. It doesn't matter that you don't intend her harm. The fact that you did it at all is unacceptable."

"Catching the bishop has more importance than obeying social norms."

"You mean laws."

"Those too. We don't have time to debate issues of morality."

"Issues of morality remain the only thing separating us from the evil we fight against."

The basement had a deadbolt on this side, but the handle didn't have a lock of its own. Niccolo wrenched it open and headed down the stairs. Arthur followed behind, but the Hunter made no move to stop him.

"A much greater divide exists than you might imagine, and stopping to consider what you *will* and *will not* do to achieve your mission offers the quickest way to an early grave."

It looked dim inside the basement with only a single overhead light. Niccolo held the handrail as he rushed down the risers. Only a small window led to the outside world from down here, far too small for even a small child to fit through.

Three small prison cells lined the walls of the basement, each about ten feet wide and with several feet of separation between them. The bars all seemed heavy and made of metal and appeared relatively new.

Inside one of the cells sat a middle-aged woman, dirty and disheveled. If Niccolo had to guess, she hadn't slept in days. She stared at the floor but climbed to her feet when she saw Niccolo standing at the bottom of the stairs.

"Thank God!" she said. "Please, can you help me ..."

Her voice trailed off, though, and a moment later, her eyes went wide with fear.

Niccolo thought, at first, that she'd spotted Arthur on the staircase behind him, but then realized she looked directly at him.

"You're not …?" She looked at Arthur. "He's not …?"

"He isn't with the bishop." Arthur stepped forward to stand alongside Niccolo. He held up his hands in a non-threatening manner, trying to calm her.

"But, he's with the Church!"

"He didn't even *know* Bishop Glasser," Arthur said. "And, like me, he wants to stop him from hurting anyone else."

"What is she talking about?" Niccolo asked, completely caught off-guard by her response. He turned to her. "What do you mean?"

The woman jerked back when he spoke to her. Arthur tapped his shoulder and gave a curt shake of his head. Niccolo took a step back from the cell, and then turned to the woman.

"I'll get you out of here. I promise."

She backed away, shaking her head and still looking terrified. "I don't want anything from you. Please go. Please, just go!"

Her outburst took Niccolo by surprise, but he did as she said. He backed up toward the stairs, walking slowly, and then rushed all the way up. Arthur followed, and a moment later, they stood in the living room.

Arthur shut the door behind them, bolted it, and then headed toward the sofa.

"I suspected she wouldn't feel too happy to see you," Arthur said, "but I didn't anticipate *that* response. It confirms a lot of my suspicions."

"What the hell just happened?" Niccolo asked, bewildered.

"She wasn't the bishop's accomplice," Arthur said. "She was his plaything. His victim."

"What? That's crazy."

"It's true. The bishop spent years mistreating her and

ruining her life before he ever started his attack on Everett. It started when she was a little girl."

Niccolo couldn't believe what Arthur told him. "No, no, that's not right. That can't be right."

"It's true."

"If something like that had happened, she should have reported it to the Church."

Arthur stared at him. "She did. Multiple times. Why do you think she has so much fear of you?"

The words hit like a sucker punch to Niccolo's gut. He sat in an armchair, staring at the fireplace and trying to absorb what Arthur had said.

"To her, you are just another priest here to abuse her."

The idea that the bishop could do something like this—like *this*—to someone ...

Niccolo took a deep and steadying breath. The thing was, honestly, it didn't seem that hard to believe once the initial shock went away. It came down to more just a fact of seeing firsthand the terror of what the bishop could do to an innocent person. Niccolo had known he was an evil man, and this just brought another atrocity to add to the list.

But the idea that Desiree had gone to the Church for help, and they'd let her down like this ...

"You brought her here because of me," Niccolo said, suddenly, an insidious thought worming its way into his mind. "You wanted *me* to see her, and you wanted her to see me."

"Yes."

"You won't even try to deny it? You wanted to manipulate me. You planned to turn me against the Church."

"Never," Arthur said. "I wanted to open your eyes to the world around you."

"You think I don't know about evil? I went to Everett, too."

"I think facing an evil demon and facing an evil person are two entirely separate things. One is evil because of its nature, but the other chooses to be that way. I needed to make sure you were up to the challenge of facing the bishop."

"And what is your assessment?" Niccolo asked bitterly.

Arthur studied him for a moment. "That yet remains to be seen. However, that wasn't the only reason I brought her here. I truly do think she might have valuable information we can use to find Leopold."

"What information? She's a victim."

"It's a long shot, but she provides the only lead we have."

"And, has she turned up anything?"

"Not yet."

"Then, let her go."

"I can't."

Niccolo had never felt so furious and confused in his entire life. "You told me that if I helped you, we wouldn't hurt people. That *you* wouldn't hurt people. You swore to me that you had changed."

"I swore to you that I *would* change. And I have. I haven't harmed her, and I won't harm her. I haven't even scared her," Arthur said. "And I don't intend to. You have my word that as soon as we deal with the bishop, and have him safely in the Vatican's custody, I will return her to her home."

"Then, why not now?"

"She won't be safe."

"What do you mean?"

"I mean that when I kidnapped her, I didn't know if she had information against the bishop, and I doubt he does either. He probably thinks she's a liability."

"So?"

"We exposed the bishop and sent him on the run in Everett, and now he knows about us searching for him. If Desiree knows something about him that could help us catch him, then what's the first thing *he* would do to her when she got home?"

Niccolo's eyes widened. "He would kill her?"

"Bingo, and if only to tie up loose ends," Arthur said. "I didn't have a choice. If I hadn't kidnapped her, the bishop might have killed her when he realized the letters remained in his manor. If we let her leave now, he most certainly will, if only to punish her for speaking with us."

Niccolo felt backed into a corner. On the one hand, what Arthur had done infuriated him, and he believed with all his heart that it was a wrong and horrible thing to do ...

But, on the other hand, it made sense, if only from Arthur's perspective. Arthur had certainly taken a lot of liberties in his assessment, but it remained possible he had it right.

The thing was, it also terrified him to think of things from Arthur's perspective. Niccolo hadn't yet grown used to thinking so poorly of people, and for certain, he didn't enjoy trying to imagine the things someone like the bishop might do to keep them from finding him.

It gave yet another reminder that this wasn't his world.

As much as he hated it, Niccolo could do nothing about this situation. Still, he didn't think Arthur had it right, and he felt the man had got it wrong when he kidnapped her to begin with, but what was done was done. He stood and walked back toward the basement.

"Where are you going?" Arthur stood and moved to follow. Niccolo held up a hand to stop him.

"I'm going to talk to her alone. You kidnapped her, so we might as well make the best of the situation we find ourselves in."

"I told you. I questioned her already. She doesn't know anything."

"I have no intention of questioning her about anything."

"Then, what? Why do you want to talk to her?"

Niccolo stopped at the basement door and looked back at Arthur. "You said that she came to the Church for help on multiple occasions and that we turned her away."

Arthur hesitated, and then nodded. "Yes. That's what

she told me."

"Then I'll go and apologize to her and beg for forgiveness."

"It wasn't your fault," Arthur said. "You didn't even know her or her situation."

"I'm a servant of God," Niccolo said. "And a servant of the Church. It was my duty to protect her, and my duty to know."

✳✳✳

As he came down the stairs, Niccolo heard the woman sobbing. He didn't know what he would say to her, but he had to say something. Or, at the very least, he had to listen.

He strode across the dim room and stopped next to her cell. His hands shook, and in many ways, this felt worse than when he'd gone into the home of Rose Gallagher to face the demon. Desiree didn't look up at him, just kept sobbing, and the sound of her cries broke his heart.

He refused to be the first to speak, allowing the silence to drag on. Instead, he simply stood there, waiting. Maybe she didn't even know he stood there; a long few minutes passed before she spoke. "Why ... why are you doing this?"

"Arthur ... *we* just want to keep you safe."

She chuckled sardonically, glancing up at him from the cot. "Safe? Since when does anyone care if I'm safe?"

Niccolo didn't have a good answer. "I care," he said. "I feel impossibly sorry for what has happened to you."

"You? Sorry? It's a little late for that."

"I know. The Church failed you, and as a representative of the Church, I want to offer you my deepest condolences and apology."

She didn't respond, just looked back at the floor. Then she said, "Thanks."

"I know it doesn't mean much, but—"

"I said thanks. And I'm sorry about earlier. I just ... it's been a long day."

"Tell me about it," Niccolo said. "I've spent all day driving."

"Your accent—are you Italian?"

"I am. Born in Rome and lived much of my life in the Vatican."

She nodded. "I never made it to Italy. Always wanted to go, just never worked out."

He didn't know how to respond to that without useless platitudes. They stood in awkward silence for a minute. Finally, Niccolo changed the subject.

"Arthur said he spoke to you about the bishop?"

"He did. He is quite direct."

"Did he behave cruelly to you?"

She shook her head. "No. But, as I told him, I don't know the bishop's whereabouts. I don't know *anything*. I haven't spoken to Leopold in months. I thought maybe I had broken free of him and that, maybe, he had *finally* let me go when *this* happened."

"Do you still have the letters he sent?" Niccolo asked. "We only saw your letters, not the ones he sent to you."

"I destroyed them," the woman said. "He made me swear I would get rid of them. Occasionally, he would send his goons to check. It all just meant a game to him. I gave him something just to pass the time."

"I'm sorry."

She chuckled. "What good is your sorry to me now? What the hell do you care? I've spoken to many priests. They fall into two groups: one wants to tell me sorry, and the other wants me to tell *him* sorry. All they ever cared about was making sure I didn't speak to the press."

"I *am* sorry. I truly am. If I had known ..."

She waved her hand, cutting him off. "If you had known, you would have done nothing. No one ever does anything, and that's just how it is. It'll stay like this forever, and nothing will ever change."

"There are good people out there."

"Good priests, you mean? Of course, there are. But also bad ones. You can tell yourself that they cancel each other out, but when all I've ever seen are the bad ones … you might be a good guy, but forgive me for not wanting to find out. Please, just leave me alone."

Niccolo frowned deeply. He wanted to fix this problem, to solve it, but realized just how deep it went. Bishop Glasser had ruined this woman's entire life. No words or gestures would solve that.

Not unless he could give Desiree back her life.

"I'll return," he said, finally. "To speak with you. If that is all right with you."

She waved her hand. "I don't know anything."

"Not for that. Just to speak with you."

"Not like I have a choice."

"Yes," he said. "You do. If you would prefer that I never return, then you will not see me again. But, I would like to, if that's okay?"

She hesitated, and then shrugged. "Suit yourself."

"Do you feel hungry?"

"A bit," she said. "Your friend has only given me disgusting food, though."

Niccolo half-smiled. "I feel certain that's all he has. Would you like anything in particular?"

She hesitated, and then said, "Chicken? Real stuff, not from a can."

"I'll see what I can do."

He turned to leave and sensed the woman come up to the bars behind him. She reached through and grabbed his shirt, though she did it gently. He turned to face her.

"Please, I know he's your friend, but I just want to go home."

Niccolo promised, "You will. I swear to you that we will stop the bishop, and then we will get you safely back home. You have my word."

Then he turned and hurried back up the stairs before the woman could say anything else. He felt horrible, leaving her trapped in a cell like this, and realized that he ran away from himself as much as from her.

Two weeks ago, before he went to the town of Everett, Washington, he would have called the police immediately if he saw a situation like this. At the least, he would have let Desiree loose and helped her escape from the cabin. It seemed like something from a horror movie, and he would have reported Arthur to the proper authorities to get dealt with.

But, in the last two weeks, his entire world had flipped on its head. Arthur remained a dangerous and rash person, and at one point, Niccolo had believed him to be evil as well.

Not anymore, though.

Now, he knew true evil.

Problematically, he had also learned that a lot of gray areas existed in the world. More than he had imagined. He had thought that he would help Arthur in bringing down the bishop without compromising any of his convictions.

Arthur had brought Desiree out here to disabuse him of that notion, and had done it on the first night. If that spoke about how the rest of their partnership would go, then Niccolo had to admit to more than a small reservation.

"We will return her home safely," Niccolo said to Arthur as he bolted the basement door once more. "As soon as this has finished, we will get her home."

"Of course we will," Arthur said. "I'll drop her off back in her bed as though nothing ever happened, and she will *never* have to hear from the bishop or us ever again. She can go on with her life."

"What life?" Niccolo shook his head. "I ... I can't believe what she's endured already."

"In my experience, the people who endure the worst things in life also endure the most. It isn't fair, but it is what it is."

"Her family must know she's missing."

"She has little. I planted some clues, and they think she went out for a few weeks' vacation and don't expect her back anytime soon. We've got eight more days before they'll start to worry or contact the police."

Niccolo shook his head. He felt shocked, and a little scared, at how methodical Arthur was about all of it.

"I can't believe you could do something like this."

"Can't you?" Arthur asked. He walked back into the kitchen. "I feel pretty sure that this is tame compared to what you can *imagine* me doing. Or what I've done. You, more than most, know my capabilities."

He spoke the last slowly, the words barely audible, and Niccolo could see regret in his eyes. What he said was true: Arthur held responsibility for killing more than twenty people in West Virginia not even a year earlier. The worst part was that it didn't even scratch the top of whatever else Arthur had done.

They were all cultists working for a dangerous and psychotic organization known as The Ninth Circle that kidnapped and murdered at will, but that didn't change what Arthur had done.

Niccolo had helped the Church to hide what had happened from the rest of the world. They buried the bodies, cleaned up the old manor, and quieted news outlets and media.

All in the name of the greater good.

He had hated Arthur ever since it had happened, but that came before the Church had called him out for the fateful events in Everett. Even after everything that had happened, though, he still wouldn't have worked with Arthur except he felt that Arthur harbored remorse for what he had done and wanted to change.

Or, at least, he pretended to change, and he made an excellent actor.

"It is still wrong," Niccolo said. "Perhaps I made a mistake in coming here. If this is how you plan to do things …"

Arthur held up a hand, silencing him. "That is how *we* plan to do things," he said. "A line in the sand lays between all the decent people out there in the real world and the people like me. If you're to help me bring down the bishop, then you *will* cross that line. Once you do, there's no going back. And bringing Desiree here is tame compared to what we might be forced to do in this hunt, and I need to know that you won't get in my way. Are you an asset or a liability? Can you handle this?"

"Handle what? You talked about a line in the sand, but I see one line I *will* not cross."

"What line?"

"I won't help you kill people."

"I have no intention of murdering anyone," Arthur said. "Not ever again. That Arthur has gone. But we might need to do terrible things if we're to stop Leopold, and this only makes the first. If you don't feel okay with that, then you should get back in your car and head on down the road."

Niccolo stood there for a long moment, trying to reconcile the good that he would do by helping bring down the bishop with the bad of which Arthur asked him to become a part. A fragment of him felt furious with Arthur, knowing that the woman in the basement was only a distraction and test for him.

The rest of him, though, knew that Arthur had it right about everything. Arthur asked him to cross a line and join him in the gray areas of the world. Truthfully, he had crossed that line the moment he entered the home of Rose Gallagher back in Everett and exorcised the demon possessing her. He had crossed over into another world, a darker world, and nothing in his life would ever be the same.

"Doing this," he said slowly. "Hunting down the bishop ... it doesn't mean we have to compromise who we are. I won't just do anything without a good reason."

"No," Arthur said. "But if you're unwilling or unable to do the necessary, then you will get us both killed. I need to know that I can trust you out there when it counts."

Niccolo took a deep breath and nodded. "Very well. I'm committed to doing this."

"Are you? I want you to take some time and ask yourself that question seriously, because you cannot come half-committed to something like this. You are either all in, or you are all out—straddling the line isn't a good place to be."

Niccolo opened his mouth, but Arthur raised his hand again to cut him off.

"I'm serious. Think on it. It's late, and we've both grown exhausted. Give it some thought and bring me your decision tomorrow."

"Okay."

"If I don't see you when I get up, then I'll know what you decided and will hold no hard feelings. However, if you do decide to stick around and help me bring down the bishop, then don't ever again question me about things like this."

Then, before Niccolo could respond, Arthur turned and headed out the back door of the cabin and into the cold night air. Niccolo stood there, watching him disappear, lost in his thoughts.

Not for the first time, he wondered just what the hell he had gotten himself into.

Chapter 3

Niccolo didn't leave.

It pleased Arthur quite a bit when he awoke the next morning and found Niccolo sitting in the living room. More than he would like to admit, in fact. Though confident that he could catch and deal with the bishop one way or another, having someone around brought a nice benefit.

In particular, having Niccolo around. Arthur had worried that Niccolo would leave in the middle of the night. It wouldn't have surprised him, and to be honest, it might have turned out for the best. His next steps in hunting down the bishop would bring danger, and it certainly fell outside of Niccolo's world. Usually, Arthur worked alone, yet he had to admit that, sometimes, it felt nice to have help.

But, it came down to more than that. Niccolo Paladina, a few years older than Arthur, brought a calm maturity about the world in ways that made him seem a lot older. He had become, in many ways, Arthur's newfound conscience— his voice of reason—in the new life Arthur tried to create for himself.

The priest sat on one of the couches with a Bible open on his lap. He appeared exhausted, and Arthur knew he wouldn't have slept much, if at all. Though still going, the fireplace had burned down to almost nothing. Instead, Niccolo sat wrapped in blankets dragged from his room.

When Arthur came into the room, he glanced up and folded the book closed on his lap. Arthur waited for him to say something, but he didn't. Instead, they just stared at each other until the silence became awkward.

"Would you like some tea?" Arthur asked, finally, heading to the kitchen. He filled up a kettle and set it on the stove. To light the burner, he had to use matches and had run low. Later, he would need to stock up on supplies.

"No, thank you." Niccolo set the book on the couch next to him.

"Coffee, then?"

"No."

"You should get some caffeine," Arthur said. "Doesn't look like you got much rest, and we'll have a long day."

"I thought you said we didn't have any leads to follow up on."

"We don't," Arthur said. "Not yet, at least. But we'll still be busy."

"Doing what?"

"Training. We won't leave this cabin until I have confidence you can take care of yourself and won't panic at the first sign of trouble."

Arthur grabbed a loaf of bread out of one of the cupboards and sliced off a few pieces. They had grown hard and stale, but better than nothing. At least they hadn't yet gone moldy. He turned on another burner, grabbed the slices with tongs, and heated them up.

"No toaster?"

"The generator isn't running. We only have the gas burners."

"Ah."

"Food is food."

"So you keep telling me," Niccolo said. "Yet, I still can't help but disagree."

"You'll get used to it."

"Maybe. What kind of training did you have in mind?"

Arthur finished toasting the bread and then grabbed a jar of grape jelly from the cabinet. He brought that, two cups of coffee, and the slightly burnt bread into the living room and sat down across from Niccolo.

"Eat."

"I'm not hungry."

"I don't care. Eat."

Reluctantly, Niccolo picked up some of the bread. He took a bite.

"No jelly?" Arthur asked.

"I prefer jam."

"You won't find any jam here," Arthur said. "This is a jam-free zone."

"What training?"

Arthur finished smearing about half of the jar onto his toast and then took a bite. "Have you ever fired a gun before?"

"I told you, I'm not—"

"The tranquilizer dart guns that I acquired are similar to normal pistols, though lighter and with only three darts. They're also extremely expensive, so I expect a fair amount of accuracy from you if you're to carry one."

"I don't intend on carrying one."

"And I don't intend on you leaving this cabin without one. You might as well just accept it and learn how to shoot."

"And how do you plan on me learning that? I've never been a fighter and don't know how to use a gun."

"Guns don't require you to be a fighter. Pretty much, they prove the antithesis to it. You aim and pull the trigger."

"I don't think that will be—"

"This isn't up for debate," Arthur said. "You *will* learn how to shoot a tranquilizer gun, and you *will* figure out how to hit your target before we leave this cabin."

Niccolo leaned forward and stared at Arthur, his frustration and anger palpable. Had he pushed Niccolo too far? The priest's expression looked unreadable, and a long while passed before he spoke.

"Fine."

"Good."

"We will let Desiree train as well."

"Excuse me?"

"Everything you teach *me* about these tranquilizer guns, you will teach *her* as well."

"No," Arthur said, shaking his head in disbelief. "That is *not* happening."

"This isn't up for debate either. I don't appreciate getting manipulated or lied to, and you brought her here because of me."

"And to keep her safe. But, fair enough," Arthur said. "I did use her, but only to make a point."

"Consider your point made. Now, let me make mine. You said she can't defend herself, so teach her. Since you brought her here, then you will show her how to protect herself when you show me."

"You have a flaw in your logic," Arthur said. "If I show her how to use one of these guns, she can just use them on *us*."

"Then, I suppose it's a good thing you're not killing people anymore, isn't it? You'll just wake up with a really bad headache."

Arthur sat in stunned silence, fighting down the urge to yell as well as the urge to laugh. He had to admit, he felt impressed. After what he had put Niccolo through, *this* didn't bring the retribution he'd expected.

It also didn't seem a terrible idea, when he thought about it. And teaching her how to defend herself would make it easier to send her back out into the world and would be good for her. It didn't feel like a good idea, either, though, as teaching one person how to become accurate with one of these guns would prove difficult enough, but two amateurs ...

Plus, if Desiree did turn out as the sort of person to hold a grudge, he would have to keep a constant eye on her so that she didn't run away or try to shoot him.

Still, considering what he'd put them both through, it would be a small concession to make.

"Fine."

"Make no mistake, the only reason I'm still here is because you told me you intended to change your ways and that you were done murdering. The world is a dangerous place, considerably more so than I might have known during my life at the Vatican, but that does not, and will not, *ever* justify murder. Those are my terms."

"I agree to them."

"You were a murderer," Niccolo continued bluntly.

"And there is no changing that. What you've done is terrible, and maybe even unforgivable in God's eyes. The Bible teaches us, however, that *no* person falls beyond redemption, and no crime too great for forgiveness. I don't know if I believe you are redeemable, but that lies between you and God. I will work with you, Arthur, provided your change is real and permanent. However, the very *second* I decide that it isn't, I will work to stop you and make you pay for all your crimes."

Arthur leaned back in his chair. "Fair enough."

Niccolo set the book on the table next to him. "Then, since we have that settled, what do we do next?"

"Now," Arthur said, standing up and brushing the crumbs from his hands. "We get to work."

✳✳✳

Arthur headed out to get the range ready for their target practice while Niccolo disappeared into the basement to gather up Desiree Portman. He doubted she would want to participate, and he didn't blame her. If she proved unwilling, he wouldn't force her. He had no idea what the priest intended to say to her to convince her to participate, and he just hoped the priest didn't get his hopes up about his grand scheme.

However, they both emerged from the front door of the cabin about ten minutes later, Niccolo leading Desiree out to the range where Arthur stood waiting. She looked skittish and wary, as if ready to bolt at a moment's notice, but she also looked confused.

Arthur waited patiently for them both to make it out to him, raising an eyebrow at Niccolo. He felt impressed that Niccolo had convinced her to come. However, that didn't mean he would trust her, nor her intentions, outright—after all, he *did* kidnap her. The priest nodded at him, and he cleared his throat.

"First things first," Arthur said. "We are a long way from

any cities and surrounded by dangerous terrain and animals. And running away will only get you killed."

Niccolo sighed. "We're here to help her, not scare her."

"I am helping," Arthur said. "I'm just stating the facts so that no one gets hurt." Then he reached behind him on the table and picked up one of the tranquilizer guns. He only had two of them and about sixty darts.

"These," he said, holding up the gun so that they could see it, "shoot tranquilizer darts. Each holds three darts, and each dart holds enough horse tranquilizer to take down a bull in a couple of seconds."

He handed the first one to Niccolo. The priest held it gingerly, like it was a snake that might bite him. He handed the second one to Desiree, and her eyes went wide in shock. Arthur could see the thoughts running through her head as she realized it was loaded.

"Both of them," he said quickly. "Are fully loaded, but right now, I only have water in them to simulate the weight of a real dart."

Her face fell, and she lowered the gun to her side.

For the next twenty minutes, Arthur walked then through how the guns worked. He showed them how to take them apart and put them back together and explained their inner workings. Squat cartridges in the back made them bulky and released the compressed air that propelled the darts. After ten or so shots, they would need to pop out the old one and put in a new canister to keep firing.

It made the entire process cumbersome and slow, but they remained some of the best and most accurate dart guns on the market. Arthur had researched them and found these to be cutting edge, but the technology still hadn't become that portable. The problem was, they could never offer a suitable substitute for a real gun, especially with their cost.

Finally, they began their target practice. Arthur started with a quick demonstration on how to hold the gun and how to aim, firing three darts into the chest of his target. The other two watched him studiously, and then they had a go at shooting as well.

It proved abysmally bad.

Niccolo fired the first three shots clean over the target and past the mammoth backstop that Arthur had erected, sending the darts sailing somewhere into the woods behind it. There seemed almost no way they would manage to track them down, which meant a lot of lost money. Desiree did better, managing to hit the target with one shot and the backstop with the other two.

Arthur bit back a groan and headed off into the woods to attempt to retrieve the missing darts. He doubted he would find them, but he didn't have any choice but to try. They cost a lot of money, after all.

✳✳✳

After a few hours of shooting, they stopped for a break. Niccolo had improved his accuracy, able to hit the backdrop consistently, and occasionally, the target, but he remained a long way from being ready to use the dart gun in combat.

That didn't make the point of the exercise anyway. Best case scenario, Niccolo would never have to fire the dart gun or any gun in their time together. If things went well, then Niccolo would, basically, just carry a backup weapon for him.

Arthur used the training opportunity to further test Niccolo. Get him outside his comfort zone and see how he responded. Would he close up and shut down when things didn't go his way, or would he respond well and keep his focus?

So far, Niccolo had done the latter, which gave encouragement. He approached the task with determination and even seemed to have a little bit of fun with it.

Desiree barely spoke a word the entire time that they stood out at the range and seemed more depressed than interested in learning about the tranquilizer guns. That didn't surprise Arthur since he hadn't expected her to trust him after everything that had happened.

She took it in stride, though, and even seemed to warm up by the end of their morning session. She would answer him politely and managed to hit the target fairly often.

When they took a break, he prepared a lunch for them of canned stew and more stale bread and brought it into the living room. Desiree accepted hers and took it out onto the porch. Arthur allowed her to go, fairly certain she wouldn't try to run.

"She doesn't like you very much," Niccolo said as they sat down to eat.

"Thanks for stating the obvious. Would you?"

"Of course not," Niccolo said. "Though, I thought she would become more receptive once she found out we planned to put an end to Bishop Glasser's tyranny."

Arthur took a bite of his stew. "Most probably, she doesn't believe we will."

"She thinks we're lying?"

"More likely incompetent."

"What do you mean?"

"Think of it from her perspective: she came forward to the Church to tell the truth, and the Church completely ignored her. Worse, they called her a liar to protect an evil priest who has now become a bishop. In her eyes, the Church is, at best, incompetent and, at worst, evil."

"So, you think that she thinks we're not being honest with her?"

"Why would she believe otherwise? I'm sure countless people have promised to help her only to betray her in the end. More than that, she understands maybe even more than we do just how bad the bishop really is. She might simply think we won't manage to stop him."

Niccolo sat in silence for a long few moments. While absorbed in his thoughts, he ate a spoonful of his stew. Arthur felt somewhat surprised that Niccolo hadn't attempted to rationalize, justify, or make excuses for what the Church had done.

Maybe they didn't have enough evidence, or the woman's narrative was unreliable. Maybe they had reason to suspect she had lied. There were reasons—albeit poor ones—that Niccolo could have brought up to explain it all away, but he didn't.

It must have been difficult for him to listen to accusations like this against his beloved Church. He had dedicated his life to serving the Vatican, and this woman represented a tremendous failing of the Church to protect its people. However, he didn't even attempt to deny the accusations. Instead, he seemed more concerned with what had happened to Desiree and where to go from here.

"She might think this is one of the bishop's tests," Niccolo said, finally. "He forced her to write letters and tortured her for years. Maybe she thinks he orchestrated the kidnapping and that this is just another situation where she's supposed to prove her loyalty to him."

Arthur hadn't thought of that possibility, but it might hold truth. Desiree had no way of knowing that the bishop had gone on the run for real, and the details could fit ways he'd acted previously. "Could be."

"In which case, maybe she *does* know something and feels afraid to tell us because he would punish her."

Arthur hesitated, and then said, "No. I talked to her at length. I don't think she knows anything."

"With the life she's lived, she'd probably get quite good at pretending. She fears you, but no doubt she feels more afraid of *him*. After years of torture, if she thinks this is one of his tests, then no way would she tell you anything."

"It's possible. Unfortunately, we can't do much about it. I did sort of kidnap her, and no matter how many times I promise I'm not working with the bishop, she will never believe me."

"I can talk to her."

"You think she will believe you?"

"No," Niccolo said. "But if she knows anything at all,

then we need to at least try.”

Arthur nodded. “It sounds like a good plan. Try to win her over, and I’ll stay out of the way. Just try to get her to believe that any information she gives you, we will use to put the bishop away. We can keep her safe but only if we can find the bishop.”

“Can we, though?”

“Can we what?”

“Can we keep her safe?”

“We will bring the bishop to justice, and once he’s safely locked away in the Vatican, she’ll be free of him.”

“What if she helps us, and we fail to stop the bishop? Then, we’ll have asked her to increase her risk while she remains in danger.”

“We will.”

“But what if we don’t?”

“You overthink things.” Arthur shook his head. “We don’t have time to stop and worry about what might go wrong. We just need to deal with what we have, and right now, we have her. She gives us an asset, and brings the only clear link we have to the bishop, and if you can’t get her to talk, then our entire mission might die before it begins.”

He’d told a lie, at least partly. Arthur also pursued other avenues to find out where Bishop Glasser might have hidden out, but they would prove considerably more dangerous and problematic than if Desiree had information.

He hadn’t thought that Niccolo could get anything out of her, but if that possibility existed, it would be worth a lot. Their tenuous position would become much more solid if Niccolo managed to get the woman to divulge any relevant information.

“Fine,” Niccolo said, standing up from the couch. “I’ll try to talk to her.”

“Okay.”

Niccolo hesitated in the living room for a moment longer before heading for the exit that led out through the front door of the cabin. With one last meaningful look toward Arthur, he opened it and disappeared outside.

Arthur watched him go, and then leaned back on the couch. It impressed him that Niccolo had the willingness to address the problem head-on, and Arthur grew hopeful that he might manage to get some information ... but he also didn't get his hopes up too high. He had spoken to Desiree extensively when he'd first kidnapped her, and even though it remained possible that Niccolo had it correct about her motivations, it seemed significantly more likely that she simply didn't know anything of use.

The bishop stayed careful and guarded, and the likelihood that he would slip up and give important information to a victim didn't appear that plausible.

Still, it seemed better than nothing.

Plus, it would give him a chance to further evaluate Niccolo before they headed out into the dangerous real world. He needed to see the priest's capabilities and hoped Niccolo would turn out as a resourceful and valuable companion in all of this, and only time would tell.

Chapter 4

Niccolo found Desiree out on the front porch with a sad look on her face as she stared off into the distance. She twirled her stew with her spoon, but it looked like she'd eaten little of it.

When he walked over toward the rocking chair where she sat, she glanced up, but her gaze shifted away once more. She looked broken and world-weary, and he felt horrible for her.

He felt unsure what, exactly, had prompted his ultimatum earlier that Arthur teach her to fire the guns as well. Part of it was simply because he'd grown frustrated that Arthur had manipulated him. Tired of letting Arthur control the situation, he wanted to demand something out of what unfolded.

However, the more he thought of it, the happier he became with his decision. It made him feel more in control of what happened, and it served the same purpose for Desiree. People had dealt with her horribly —particularly men—her entire life. It started with the bishop, but now Arthur had kidnapped her. Training her to shoot gave her a tool to protect herself against something like this in the future.

At least, that became his hope.

If nothing else, it got her out of the cell and into the fresh mountain air, and he hoped she at least got something from the activity of firing the guns.

He enjoyed it and found something pleasant about firing the tranquilizer darts. It gave no satisfying concussion like shooting a real weapon—they sounded more like opening a fizzy beverage than a gunshot—but it brought a nice feeling to see himself progress and accomplish something.

Niccolo glanced around for somewhere he could sit. A couple more rocking chairs sat nearby, off to the left, and he dragged one over to the door so that it rested close to hers.

"Do you mind?"

Desiree looked over at him but didn't say anything. He took her silence as assent and sat on the chair, folding his hands in his lap. Then, he just waited, having no idea what to say to the woman to get her to open up and talk to him

She didn't like him and definitely didn't trust him. He wouldn't have trusted himself either if he found himself in her position. Whether or not she believed this was some trick orchestrated by the bishop, she remained in a terrible situation.

Part of him still thought it the wrong decision to keep her here. He could give her the keys to his rental vehicle, he realized, and with a little bit of guidance, she would find her way back to civilization. The keys lay in his pocket right then, and he could hand them over and let her go. Arthur wouldn't like that decision, but he didn't much care.

He didn't, though. Too many things could go wrong. She could bring the cops back, or she might make it home and find someone waiting for her to punish her. Either case would end badly for them, but they would also end badly for her.

But, it still struck him as wrong. Niccolo had to reconcile himself with that fact and had begun to understand that everything in life was just a slippery slope. Once he made a poor decision, then he could make more poor decisions too easily to rationalize and justify that first decision.

He would do everything in his power to make amends for all of this once it was over, including finding the priests who had worked to cover up Bishop Glasser's actions and seeing to it that they got punished, but right now, he couldn't let Desiree go.

Even if it felt like the wrong thing, he couldn't let her leave.

He had crossed a line, he realized, and this would prove the first of many if he were to keep working with Arthur.

"A lovely day," he said.

"Is it?" she asked with a hint of bitterness. "I hadn't noticed."

"I understand. How ... how are you handling all of this?"

At first, Niccolo didn't think she would answer. It felt like a hollow question, and one he didn't have any right to ask. She sat in the chair, rocking gently and staring forward.

Finally, she spoke, "Not that well. I thought Leopold had left my life forever when he stopped sending me those letters. I believed I could move on. He would call me sometimes, too. He would ask how I was doing and make me promise I missed him. Usually, I couldn't sleep for a week after those calls. And yet, finally, I thought it was over. I should have known better. I suppose this is just more of the same."

"This isn't more of the same. I promise you that. We're here to stop him and stop what he's doing to you."

"I've heard that so many times before," she said. "All I got for my troubles was mockery and disdain. My family won't even speak to me anymore because of the things I said against the Church when I thought people were here to help. They don't even believe me and call me a liar and worse. After a while, I just gave up and did whatever Leopold asked of me. It seemed ... easier."

"The things he did to you ..." Niccolo shook his head, finding out that he couldn't continue the thought aloud.

He had meant to call them unspeakable acts that no person should ever do to another, let alone a priest, but the words stuck in his throat. Just imagining the way Desiree had been tortured and mistreated horrified him.

This didn't resemble anything he had faced in Everett when the possessed townspeople tried to kill him. It wasn't like the demon living inside of Rose like a parasite. Those had all been good people unable to control themselves in a terrible situation. That came down to evil, but evil he could understand and do battle against.

In this case, everything Leopold had done to Desiree, he had done intentionally and personally. He had done it with the blessing and at the behest of the Church simply by their unwillingness to stop him. What he did had nothing to do with some demonic force rising up to harm someone. What he did lay in his true nature as a human being.

This seemed much, much worse.

"I need to stop him," Niccolo said.

"Why?"

The question caught him off-guard, and he fumbled for an answer. He hadn't even thought up a good reason for why he needed to bring the bishop to justice but had just accepted as self-explanatory.

"Because what he is doing is wrong and terrible."

"Why now? What about what he did *before*? Why has the Church just now become interested in bringing him to justice? What has he done now that warrants your attention?"

Niccolo thought over his response carefully. "He deals with forces outside his control. Things he doesn't understand."

"So, now you want to stop him?"

"We *need* to stop him. What he has embarked upon is terrible and evil."

"What he did to me was terrible and evil," Desiree said, with that hint of bitterness creeping back into her tone. "What made *that* any different?"

Niccolo didn't have a good answer. He had entered dangerous territory in the conversation. If he admitted that his reason for stopping the bishop came purely because of what had happened in Everett, then he risked cheapening everything she had experienced. But, in many ways, that showed the exact truth of things.

It felt dirty even to him that the only time someone came wanting to stop the bishop happened when he dabbled in the paranormal, and not when he mistreated children.

"I'm sorry."

"So, when he only abused *me* and the others like me, then everything was fine and dandy, but now that other people are at risk, you want to get involved."

"I didn't *know*—"

"No one ever knows," Desiree said sarcastically. She sighed. "Even when I had overwhelming evidence against him, they always just sounded shocked that I could even raise the accusation. They would whittle down my proof with lies and innuendo and then blame me for even suggesting it. No one ever listens."

"I'm listening."

"Because you *want* something from me. I can't help you. I wish I could, but not for you or me. I want to help because of all of the other people he hasn't yet hurt. I don't want him to harm anyone else, but I don't know anything."

"Maybe you know something but don't *know* you know it."

"You sound like a therapist. And a bad one at that."

Niccolo ignored the jab. "A name, maybe. Can you think of anyone the bishop mentioned in passing? There has to be someone he might have mentioned that had importance to him. A friend, maybe."

She shook her head. "I don't know *anything* at all."

Niccolo watched her for a second, and then nodded. "All right. I am sorry to pry, but it is imperative that we find him. I know you don't believe me, but I do intend to stop him, and I feel dejected for what happened to you."

"I know," Desiree said, looking back out at the woods. Her expression changed slightly. "I've been around liars enough to know one when I see one, and you don't seem like one to me."

Niccolo hesitated, surprised by the compliment. "Thank you."

"It seems quite peaceful out here."

"I agree. When I first arrived, all I could think was how terrible it was to be so far from civilization, but now ... it's amazing how fast we adapt."

"Your friend isn't exactly the friendliest person I've ever met, but he hasn't mistreated me."

"He is ... complicated," Niccolo said. That seemed the most polite word he could think of to describe Arthur.

"Most people are."

"When we get this over with, I will help you find closure for what happened to you. If you want to go after the Church for what they did to you, I will stand by you one hundred percent, even if it costs me my collar."

This time, she didn't answer at all. He realized that he had, probably, gone too far with the bold proclamation, but he stood by it. Though he might have increased his willingness to do bad things in this venture, that didn't mean he would stop doing the right thing, no matter what it cost.

Desiree turned away from him, signaling that the conversation had ended. Niccolo waited a moment longer, wondering if he should apologize, and instead, he headed back toward the door of the cabin.

"I will find Leopold," he said just before going inside. "And I *will* stop him. You have my word."

She didn't even acknowledge the words, and simply kept staring at the woods. Niccolo watched her for a moment, and then went into the cabin to find Arthur.

✳✳✳

Inside, he couldn't locate Arthur, and when Niccolo went searching for him, he found him out near the practice range once more with his tranquilizer guns. Arthur had one of the weapons in each hand and stood sighting down at a target.

This target, Niccolo noticed, lay about three times farther away than when Niccolo and Desiree had practiced. Niccolo watched while Arthur fired off six darts in rapid succession, each hitting near or on the bulls-eye.

"She doesn't know anything," Niccolo said as he walked up to the table where Arthur stood. The Hunter glanced over at him, reloading the weapon quickly with darts piled on the table. He moved with deft ease and had all six darts back into the gun in only seconds.

"I know," Arthur said. "Worth a try, though."

He sighted down the gun once more, aiming at the targets. However, he hesitated before pulling the trigger and glanced back at Niccolo.

"Do you think that if I told her she could leave but then asked her to stay that she would?"

"What?"

"I'd rather not keep her here as a prisoner. You had it right, and I would prefer to keep her as a guest than lock her in a cell. But, if I offer for her to leave and she says yes, then I won't have any choice except to keep her here."

"If you offer for her to leave but only accept one answer, then it isn't a real offer."

Arthur shrugged. "Fair enough. It's a six-hour drive to get her back home, and even if she were safe, we couldn't afford the lost time."

"Why the sudden guilt?"

"No reason," Arthur said. "I just feel bad because we kidnapped her."

"You mean *you* kidnapped her," Niccolo said.

Arthur nodded, conceding the point. "Sure. In any case, she's been missing for a few days, so Leopold has, no doubt, concluded that we're grilling her for information. Best case, he assumes she didn't tell us anything. He'll still want to talk to her to be sure, which puts her at risk. Worst case, he assumes she sold him out and will want to kill or punish her. Either way, things don't end well for her."

"So, basically, you've put her in danger by bringing her here?"

"Yes. Leopold's goons are watching her house as we speak."

"A guess?"

"I know. Frieda drove by her house this morning and saw a few men go through her house. They were checking it out and looking for her, and not to buy her lunch."

"Why didn't you tell me that before?"

Arthur shrugged. "It wasn't important."

"Of course it was. It means the risk isn't hypothetical anymore. If we tell her that, she might feel more willing to help us."

"Or she'll think we're lying."

"Hasn't she gone through enough already that we don't need to assume she's a liar?"

"Of course," Arthur said, picking up the other tranquilizer gun and handing it to Niccolo. "You're right, but all of this comes down to semantics and inconsequential details. Right now, the only thing that matters is making sure *you* get ready so that when the time comes to help her, you don't end up dead."

Niccolo stared at the offered gun but didn't take it immediately. "I don't think I'm in the mood just now."

"I don't care," Arthur said. "We've had this discussion already. If you wanted out, you missed that opportunity."

Again, he held one of the guns out to Niccolo. Hesitantly, Niccolo took it and held it at arm's length. His conscience got the best of him, as well as his guilt for what Leopold Glasser and the Church had done to Desiree. Though not his fault, he had a hard time reconciling that against what had happened to this woman her entire life.

"Fine."

"I have a few rifles as well that launch darts, but these are easier to keep with us without them being obvious."

"Where do you buy the actual tranquilizer? Isn't it regulated?"

"For use on humans, yes. I obtain it from Thoroughbred Supply Company. I just tell them that I'm a veterinarian, and they let me buy as much as I want."

"That works?"

"You would be surprised."

"How fast does it knock people out?"

"It administers instantly and takes effect in only seconds."

"You know that?"

"Personally," Arthur said. "The first thing I did was

inject myself to see how well the darts worked."

"What? Why?"

"Because I needed to be sure they would prove effective."

"What about demons?"

Arthur shrugged. "It will work on the human biology, but I have no clue if it will affect the demon. I haven't exactly had one to test it on yet."

"So, this is our plan to keep from killing people?"

"It's worth a shot. The fact that it only carries three shots is difficult to work around, but they do have fair accuracy. Plus, it's lighter than my colt and doesn't have any kick."

"Okay," Niccolo said. "So, how much more do I need to train with this before you'll consider me ready to go?"

"When you can hit the bull's-eye with every shot."

Niccolo laughed. Arthur didn't. "You're joking, right?"

"Do I look like I'm joking?"

"You never look like you're joking."

"I'm not asking you to shoot people. I just need to feel sure that you can defend yourself in case something goes wrong."

"What will go wrong?"

Arthur hesitated. "In my experience," he said. "Everything."

✳✳✳

Arthur kept him out for the next three hours, firing shots at the target dummy. Twice, Niccolo offered to go in search of Desiree to join them as well, but both times, Arthur refused. In the end, they opted to leave it up to her whether or not she wanted to join them.

After a while, she wandered out to the shooting range on her own. Whether from boredom or actual interest in learning how to shoot, they didn't know. Nor did they ask.

Arthur continued teaching them how to use and care for

the guns, and Niccolo and Desiree learned how to reload the darts quickly as well as how to replace the cartridges in under fifteen seconds. It proved difficult the first couple of times—the cartridges grew extremely cold after extended use and fit awkwardly into the grip—but after he got the hang of it, it only took a few tries to lock a new one into place.

Accuracy, though, remained a weak point for him. Niccolo shot all over the place. Sometimes he would fire off three shots and hit the bull's-eye with each one, and the next reload, all three darts would miss the target completely.

He had never done anything like this before, and he found that the timing of his breathing mattered quite a bit as to where the darts ended up. As time went on, he got better but missed the target too consistently. More than once, they found themselves out in the woods tromping around and searching for missing darts. Arthur had a large box of them, but it hadn't turned out enough, considering how bad Niccolo was.

Arthur grew more and more frustrated by Niccolo's lack of progress. By the end of the session, they had given up on recovering two of them.

However, by the end of the day, Niccolo felt quite pleased with how much better he had gotten with the dart guns.

Arthur made a half-decent meal of venison and potatoes, and Desiree ate with them in the living room. Everyone had grown exhausted, and no one spoke, but it seemed comfortable. She remained wary, especially around Arthur, but seemed more relaxed now. Niccolo couldn't help but wonder, though, if Stockholm syndrome had won her over.

Afterwards, Niccolo headed off to bed, considerably sorer than in a long while, but feeling rather good. Desiree had said it true: it was peaceful out here in the forest, tranquil and relaxing in ways he'd never experienced in Italy or the Vatican. It felt as much like he was on vacation as anything else.

Of course, with the looming specter of the bishop ever on his mind, it proved difficult to get his mind to relax.

***

The next three days brought more of the same, and after a while, it became a steady routine. Arthur awakened Niccolo early, and then they spent a few hours doing exercises—hiking, pushups, and stretches—before spending the rest of the day at the shooting range.

During that time, he learned almost nothing else about Arthur. The man remained a closed book about his past and his life before Niccolo met him and completely unwilling to talk about his family before the events in West Virginia.

However, he did learn quite a bit more about Desiree. She participated in most of what they did, and before long, she ceased to be a prisoner and became more like a compatriot in the mission against the bishop. The woman opened up to Niccolo more, talking openly about her life and family.

Arthur offered her the third small bedroom in the cabin, which she accepted graciously. No one mentioned her time in the cell or the fact that Arthur had kidnapped her.

She remained reserved around Arthur, but when just the two of them, she would speak to Niccolo about her life and the bishop. Arthur seemed to realize this and made himself scarce fairly often. He spent quite a bit of time on a satellite phone in the woods, following up on leads with Frieda and trying to figure out where they would go next. So far, nothing had panned out.

Aside from that, though, things continued quietly and peacefully. Niccolo had to admit that it was the last thing he had expected in coming out here, and he now enjoyed himself.

On that fourth night, just as he drifted off to sleep, a gentle knock sounded at his door. At first, he assumed it was Arthur, but when he opened it, Desiree stood in the hallway.

"Oh, hello," he said, rubbing his face. "Did you need something?"

"I'm sorry to disturb you," she said, "but I think I remembered a name that might be useful."

"Really?"

She hesitated. "Well, no, not a name, really. It might be nothing. Just someone he mentioned in one of his letters."

"We should find Arthur," Niccolo said.

She nodded, and they headed back toward the front of the cabin. It gave a testament to how much she trusted him now that Desiree didn't even object to that idea.

They found Arthur in the living room, staring into the fire and frowning. He stood when they approached.

"She thinks she remembers something," Niccolo said, gesturing with his hand for Desiree to sit on the couch.

"I don't know if it will help you guys find Leopold," she said. "But ..."

"Anything helps," Arthur said. "All of my contacts have turned up nothing, and the longer he's on the loose, the harder he will become to find. Leopold lives like a ghost."

"I remembered something he mentioned. Not a name, exactly, but I think it was someone he worked with."

"Who?" Arthur asked.

"A business partner he referred to as the collector."

All of the excitement drained out of Arthur's face. "A woman?"

"Yes," Desiree said, surprised. "How did you know?"

"You know who it is?" Niccolo asked. "Don't you?"

"I do." Arthur sat again and let out a sigh. "She's an old friend. I can't believe she would get caught with someone like the bishop. I also know how we can find her, but it isn't an ideal situation. I don't reckon I left on good terms the last time I went there."

"What do you mean? Who is it?"

"Naomi Develon," Arthur said.

Niccolo coughed. "Wait, what?"

"You know who she is, too?"

Niccolo hesitated for a long moment. "I don't know who the collector is, but I *know* Naomi Develon."

"How do you know her?"

"Because she works for the Church."

✳✳✳

The room fell silent for a few moments while they attempted to absorb that information. Niccolo shouldn't discuss Church business openly like this, but he realized that the danger of not telling Arthur about Naomi's relationship to the Church could prove disastrous.

"What do you mean? Naomi is a thief. Why would the Church want to work with her?"

"It's hard to explain."

"The Church pays her to steal things for them?"

"Not exactly," Niccolo said. "It's ... complicated."

"Then un-complicate it."

Niccolo hesitated, and then continued, "Yes, she works for the Church. Not stealing, though, but rather, helping us find important items. She helps us track certain ... things."

"Artifacts?"

"In a manner of speaking," Niccolo said. That was as much as he felt comfortable explaining to Arthur, so instead, he changed the subject. "You said you know of a way to find her?"

"Sort of," Arthur said with a frown. He seemed unwilling to let the issue go so easily. "What does she help the Church find?"

"Oh, you know, this and that. It doesn't matter. How do we find Naomi?"

Obviously, Arthur didn't believe him, but he decided not to press the issue. "We have to go somewhere," he said, "but, you won't like it."

Chapter 5

"Never been to a nightclub before?"

Niccolo detected a hint of jest in Arthur's tone but decided to let it slip past without comment. He couldn't—nor did he want to—hide his discomfort as they stood below the glowing neon sign that read: Afterlife.

"Of course not."

"It's an experience everyone should have at least once before they die."

"That sounds like the sort of half-witted logic an addict might use to justify their habit."

Arthur laughed. Niccolo didn't.

"Don't get too comfortable," Arthur said. "We won't stay here for long."

Niccolo scoffed at the idea—being comfortable in a place like this would prove impossible for him. As a priest, a man of the cloth, just visiting this seedy establishment, little better than a strip club, disgusted Niccolo.

Why did Arthur need him to come along, considering they'd just visited to get information? Most likely, more for Arthur's amusement than any practical reason that the man might have.

To be honest, though, it brought a nice change just to get away from the cabin for a while, even if the lead didn't pan out. He had gone a little stir crazy up there, and it felt good being back in civilization. Just that he would have preferred that the civilization didn't give an affront to his religious principles.

Of course, that assumed that he even had religious principles any longer. He'd come out here to help a Council of Chaldea Demon Hunter track down a wayward bishop, who had turned against the Church and cavorted with demons, and he did it all without the Vatican's consent.

Technically, he didn't *need* their consent, not as an anointed Exorcist, which gave him considerable leeway in such matters. Also, he rode high on his recent success in dealing with the demon crisis in Everett, but that gave only small comfort. And telling himself he didn't need approval came as nothing more than a justification for something he knew they wouldn't approve of if he asked.

They had left Desiree Portman alone at Arthur's cabin, and this time, out of the cell so that she had the run of the place. Arthur had even left her keys to a car or directions to town should she run into trouble. He had stressed, again, the importance of her not returning home, but it was anyone's guess whether she would listen.

Niccolo could tell that the situation wasn't ideal to Arthur—he had, after all, brought her to the cabin on less trusting terms—but he seemed willing to trust that she wouldn't burn down his cabin while they had gone. For what it was worth, she did seem to understand the importance of staying put and had enough canned goods and rations to keep her fed for a few months.

"This isn't a proper place for a man of the cloth."

"For some people," Arthur said with a grin, "this is where they come to pray."

"You mean prey?"

Arthur shrugged. "That too."

Heavy bass tone spilled out through the closed door, and a line of smelly and dolled-up patrons wrapped around the side of the building, waiting for their chance to gain access.

"Just stick close to me."

"I intend to."

"And don't eat or drink anything," Arthur said. "No drugs, either."

Niccolo sighed in disgust. "Let's just get this over with."

They walked up toward the front entrance of the nightclub where two bouncers blocked the line of people waiting to enter. They stood in front of a thick velvet rope and attempted to look intimidating. One a small woman, and the other a large and burly man with decidedly Italian features and a scowl on his face. Both of them frowned when Arthur walked toward them, and Niccolo could see why Arthur had said they would get a less than pleasant greeting. Clearly, they knew him.

Arthur bypassed the line altogether and walked right up to stand face-to-face with the bouncers. A few of the waiting patrons shouted or jeered at him, but he paid them no mind.

Niccolo stepped up beside him, more than a little uncomfortable in the hasty outfit Arthur had put together for him. He had traded his priestly robes and collar for a leather jacket and jeans, neither of which fit quite right. The clothes felt too tight and constricting and made him look like a fool.

"What the *hell*, Arthur?" the woman asked. "Why are you here?"

"Nice to see you, again, Carmen," Arthur said. "I need some more information. This is important."

"You can't just keep—"

"I wouldn't have come here if not for something big," Arthur said.

"You better start talking, then. Last time you came by here, you pissed off *a lot* of people. And the time before that. And so on. I didn't think you would show your ugly mug around for a long time, yet here you are."

"I don't like it any more than you."

"You'd be surprised. What do you need?"

"I need to ask Elgin a few questions."

"Or what? You'll threaten us again? This time, we have witnesses, dick."

"It's import—"

"Important, yeah, I got it. So tell me."

"It's better said in private."

"Then whisper. My hearing is real good."

Arthur stared at her for a long moment and then sighed. "Fine, Carmen, we need to know where Naomi is."

"Naomi? Naomi who?"

"Carmen …"

"What makes you think Elgin knows?"

"They are friends and go way back. He keeps her out of trouble, and she keeps him fed. Of *course* he knows where she is."

"Then, let me rephrase: why the hell would he tell you?"

"Because she's into something dangerous, and she's in way over her head. If I'm right about this, then she'll need all the help she can get not to wind up dead."

An expression flashed across Carmen's face for only a second, but Niccolo recognized it as fear and agreement. What Arthur had said had struck a chord. The expression disappeared in a heartbeat, but he knew what it meant: she worried about Naomi, even if she wouldn't admit it to Arthur.

"We want to help your friend," Niccolo said, reaching out on an impulse and touching her on the shoulder. "But we need to know where she is."

Carmen flashed him a wary look, staring at his hand like she wanted to cut it off, and then she turned back to Arthur. "Who's he?"

"Father Niccolo Paladina," Arthur said.

Carmen raised an eyebrow. "You've got to be kidding me."

Niccolo cleared his throat. "I'm afraid not. I might not have on my garbs, but I am ordained."

"Is this Church business?"

"Yes, I'm afraid so. As Arthur said, we need to speak with the proprietor of this establishment, and it is rather urgent."

Carmen thought about it a moment longer and then moved the velvet rope aside. "I'll regret this, but you've got ten minutes, Arthur. In and out, and then get the hell out of here."

"Thanks."

They moved to walk past, and then Carmen put a hand

on Arthur's chest to block him.

"He knows you're here."

"I expected as much."

"Don't get yourself shot. You bruised his ego, Arthur, so just let him have this one."

Niccolo and Arthur exchanged glances, but Arthur didn't say anything to explain Carmen's comment. Instead, he walked past the bouncers and into the nightclub.

Niccolo followed Arthur into the dimly lit and smoky building. His senses immediately became overwhelmed by the myriad sounds, colors, and closely packed bodies of the establishment main floor. Scantily clad women and men gyrated up against one another, bumping and grinding, and the entire place smelled of sweat and desperation.

Arthur forced a path through the bodies, and Niccolo struggled to keep up. The air seemed swampy and difficult to breathe. The lights disoriented him, so he focused only on watching Arthur's back as they made their way across the dance floor.

He led them over to an upward-leading staircase on the other side of the club. Metal and narrow, it had more than a few patrons standing on it, blocking their way. Arthur forced through them as well, and after a moment, they reached a second-floor ceramic walkway that encircled the building.

It led overtop and around the dance floor with a perfect view of every corner. They followed the railing to the only enclosed room in the entire club. It looked like a private office, and the door stood closed.

From this second-level vantage point, the ground floor appeared like a sea of writhing animals below. Niccolo's gaze wandered, careful not to linger on any particular gyrating body for too long. The smoke and music made him feel simultaneously alive and sick.

"I'm going to go talk to Elgin. Do you want to wait out here?" Arthur asked.

"What? Why?"

"It will get tense in there."

"What do you mean?"

"We have ... history," Arthur said. "He won't feel too happy to see me, and guns might get involved."

Niccolo hesitated. "You aren't going to ..."

"Relax. No one will get shot," Arthur said. Then, he added, "I hope."

The idea that things could get dangerous didn't come as a pleasant one for Niccolo, but the thought of staying out here on his own in the loud nightclub didn't seem ideal either.

Niccolo drew a deep and steadying breath and shook his head. "No, I'll stay with you."

Arthur studied him for a moment and then nodded. "Suit yourself."

Another bouncer waited at this door as they walked up, and he tensed when Arthur approached. A lot of people seemed to do that when Arthur was around.

"You again?" The man took a fumbling step back.

"Me again," Arthur said, stopping in front of the man and folding his hands. "Want to handle things like last time, or will you just let me in?"

"I almost lost my job because of you. You nearly broke my arm."

"*Almost* and *nearly*, huh? I'm not usually one for doing things in half-measures."

The words hung in the air. After a moment, the bouncer stepped aside and opened the door to the office behind him.

Arthur nodded at the bouncer, and then walked past and into the private room. Niccolo followed him into a darkened office space with couches and mood lighting. A large tinted window on the right side overlooked the dance floor and a stage, and expensive and comfortable chairs filled the room.

A lone man sat in one of those chairs. He held a glass of amber liquid and had a clear view of the door. Short and balding, he looked none too happy to see Arthur.

"Hello, Elgin."

"Arthur," the bald man said. "I didn't expect to see you back so soon. I trust everything worked out on your end the last time you showed up?"

"Emily is in The Council's custody. She awaits trial."

"Good for you."

"You knew that already, didn't you? You also know that I've returned to the Council's good graces, which means that this time you have an *obligation* to help me. Or do you need me to get Frieda on the line?"

"Don't berate me. Carmen let you come up here after all? She called ahead and told me you're traveling with a priest. I didn't know you had any friends."

"*Friend* is such a strong word," Arthur said. "Let's say acquaintance."

Elgin laughed. "He must not know you too well."

"On the contrary," Arthur said, still staring at the bald man. "He's one of the few that knows me probably too well. I need to know where Naomi Develon is hiding."

"Why would I know that?"

"Because, she's a collector and you are her dealer. I might not have any friends, but *you* do, and I know you've helped her."

"If you know that, then you also know that she packed up a few months ago and left town. She skipped out of here and got out of the business, as far as I know."

"No," Arthur said. "She didn't. I need to speak with her."

"About what?"

"Her newest client."

Concern flashed across Elgin's face. As with Carmen, he soon buried it beneath his cool exterior.

"Her clients are none of my business."

"This one is dangerous."

"Most of them are."

"This is different."

"I'm sorry, but I can't help you. I don't know where Naomi stays."

Arthur stood silent for a long moment, and then he let out a deep sigh. "You won't tell me?"

"I told you, I can't help."

"You want to get me to goad you, don't you?"

Elgin frowned. "Arthur ..."

"You want me to threaten you so that your goons can pop out of their hiding place behind that door over there and wave guns in my face."

"I don't know—"

"Can we skip the rigmarole and just get down to business?"

"Well, damn it, Arthur, it isn't *fun* when you don't play along."

"It isn't *fun* either way."

"Humor me."

Arthur chewed over the thought for a moment. "I guess I do deserve it, don't I?"

"And more."

In a monotone, Arthur said, "Elgin, if you don't tell me what I need to know, then I'll shoot you in the face."

"Come on." Elgin groaned. "Say it like you *mean* it."

"If you don't cut out this little song and dance, then I *will* mean it."

Elgin eyed him for a moment. "Sourpuss."

"You have my sincerest apologies."

"Stuff it. Boys."

Suddenly, a side door opened, and three men burst into the room. Two carried shotguns, and one had a pistol, and all held them trained on Arthur and Niccolo.

The entire exchange had confused Niccolo, and this downright terrified him. He stumbled backward from the door and tripped over a chair, losing his balance and nearly falling to the floor.

Elgin burst out laughing and clapped his hands. "There! At least he isn't a spoilsport."

Arthur didn't budge or take his eyes off Elgin. He stood calmly in spite of the guns aimed at his back.

"Is this necessary?"

"I learned my lesson the last time you came here, Arthur," Elgin said. "I'll not underestimate you this time."

"You also won't shoot a member of the Council, or a priest."

"Not the priest, definitely. For you, though, I might make an exception."

"Is this how you want to play things?" Arthur asked. "Do you want more injuries to explain away in the emergency room?"

"No. This isn't how I *want* to play things at all, but you haven't given me a lot of options."

"I shan't leave here without Naomi's location."

"I know. But I'll not just *give* it to you."

"What do you want?"

"I don't know who Naomi works for now, but he's not a pleasant chap. Whatever she got involved in, it isn't like her normal business, and I don't think she's doing it willingly. I need your promise that when you find her, you will let her go."

"That depends on what she has involvement in."

"No, it doesn't," Elgin said. "Not if you want her location. I want your promise. Both of you, that if you catch her, you just release."

Arthur hesitated. "That's all you want?"

"That, and a future favor when I need something."

"*This* sounds like a favor to me."

"*This* sounds like a negotiation, and I'm the one with the guns. Should I make it two extra favors?"

Arthur frowned. "Fine. We'll let her go, no questions asked, and *one* favor."

Elgin nodded and then turned his attention to Niccolo. "Your turn."

"She's a criminal. I can't make such a promise."

"Sure you can. It takes just a few simple words. Here, I'll help: I, Mr. Priest Guy, do solemnly swear ..."

"If she is guilty of a crime against the Church, then she

must receive punishment."

"Sure," Elgin said. "Just not right now. You're asking me to sell out a friend, and this is my condition."

Niccolo glanced at Arthur, who nodded almost imperceptibly. Niccolo didn't like it, but he didn't see a lot of alternatives either.

"Fine. When we find them, we'll let her go."

"Good man."

"The address," Arthur said.

"In a minute. We need to discuss one other thing." Elgin stared pointedly at Arthur. "Alone."

Arthur hesitated for a long moment, and then he glanced over at Niccolo. "Mind waiting downstairs?"

"Sure," Niccolo said.

He walked out of the room, and the guard holding the pistol followed him. The other two stayed in the office with Elgin and Arthur.

The guy following Niccolo slid the pistol away, but the look he gave him made it clear that the threat hadn't gone away with it. He gestured toward the stairwell with a look that told Niccolo to get moving. Then he followed a couple of steps behind.

The priest walked as calmly as he could down to the ground level of the building and headed toward the exit. The guy grabbed his arm, though, and dragged him toward the bar instead.

"Not just yet," the guy said.

"I'd rather wait outside."

"I'm sure you would."

Niccolo had become his prisoner, at least for the moment. He tried to pull his arm free, but the man's grip felt like iron. The guy dragged him over to the bar, and then he leaned over the counter and whistled, getting the attention of a brunette bartender. She groaned when she saw who had whistled at her, but she still came over.

"Yeah?"

"Two whiskeys," the guy said. "Make them doubles."

"You got doubles money?"

"The boss will pay for it."

She stared at him skeptically, then glanced at Niccolo. "He with you?"

"The boss said his rounds are on the house. Mine too."

"Who is he?"

"Friend of Arthur's. Shut up and pour."

She glared at him, but she did set two shot glasses on the counter. Then she filled them with amber liquid from a bottle.

When she'd finished, she attempted to put the bottle away, but the guy snatched it out of her hand and set it on the counter. The brunette stared at him for a second, and then disappeared to help more patrons.

The guy picked up the two glasses and handed one to Niccolo.

"You just wanted free drinks?"

"Shut up and drink."

"You can have mine, too."

"I wasn't asking," the guy said, pushing the drink forward again. Niccolo thought to refuse, but changed his mind almost immediately. It didn't seem like a good idea to turn the drink down at the moment.

"Salut."

They clinked the shot glasses. The guy took his down in one swallow. Niccolo tried to sip his, but the guy grabbed his hand and tilted the glass up. Some poured out of his mouth, and he coughed and sputtered when it went down his throat.

Strong stuff, it burned all the way down. Not much of a whiskey drinker back home, Niccolo preferred wine. Often, he had a glass with his meal, though this proved considerably stronger whiskey than he had grown used to. It tasted like cheap stuff with almost no flavor and a lot of kick.

It hit him instantly, making him feel fuzzy.

"What's your deal?" the guy asked when Niccolo finished sputtering. "You friends with Arthur?"

"No," Niccolo said, shaking his head. "Not exactly. Just sort of stuck working with him for now."

The guy took the shot glass back and poured out two more drinks.

"You a hunter, too?"

"No," Niccolo said. "I'm a ..."

He almost said 'priest' and then stopped himself. As part of an effort to try and blend in, he hadn't worn his collar, and giving away the fact that he worked for the Catholic Church didn't seem like a great idea right now. He had told Carmen out front, and Elgin knew, but this was different. The guy might have overheard, and he might not have; whichever, Niccolo wouldn't spell it out for him. "... just a friend," he finished unconvincingly.

The guy didn't seem to notice, or at the very least, he didn't seem to care. He handed the second full shot glass to Niccolo.

Niccolo tried again, "No, thanks."

The guy threw him a look, and Niccolo decided that one more couldn't hurt.

They downed the shots just as Arthur walked down the steps from Elgin's office. He looked amused when he spotted Niccolo standing at the counter, and then beckoned for him to head toward the exit.

The guy nodded over at him. "No explosions upstairs. Guess you're good to go."

Niccolo didn't wait a second longer. Clumsily, he dropped the shot glass onto the counter and rushed to follow Arthur. He stumbled a little from the drink and almost fell a few times, but finally, he made it to the exit and into the cool night air.

✳✳✳

"What now?" Niccolo asked as they made their way back to Arthur's car. He hiccupped and tried to cover it with a cough.

"I have a location," Arthur said. "Elgin told me a little more about the new benefactor for whom Naomi works. He doesn't know much about the guy and never met him face-to-face, but to me, it sounds an awful lot like Bishop Glasser."

A sudden burst of excitement hit Niccolo while he tried to climb into the car. The lead had paid off, and they had come another step closer to finding the bishop and making him pay for his crimes.

His body felt heavy and awkward when the alcohol took control. He moved slowly, hoping to mask his buzz. "That's good news."

"It gets better. Apparently, he got spotted with her recently and shares her hideout."

"You mean, you think we might find him there as well, wherever she has hidden out? We might actually find him with Naomi?"

"It is possible," Arthur said. "But it also solidifies my concern about their alliance."

"I know." Niccolo nodded. "I wonder if she went after the Vatican Children ..."

Niccolo trailed off when he realized he had spoken out loud. His eyes went wide, and he hiccupped. The thoughts had come to him, and the words had followed before he could stop himself. He had just said way too much.

The alcohol had numbed his ability to think straight, and he cursed himself.

Arthur climbed into the driver's seat of his rental car but didn't immediately turn it on. Instead, he stared at Niccolo with a curious expression on his face. "The Vatican Children? What do you mean?"

"Nothing, it's nothing. Never mind."

"No, it isn't. You're keeping something from me. You have done ever since you heard Naomi's name."

"No, I haven't."

"Don't lie to me, Niccolo."

He hiccupped again. "Look ... it isn't ... I mean, there's no way ..."

"Niccolo."

"Arthur, I *can't* tell you." He felt dizzy, and his head spun.

"We will not move this car until you tell me *everything* you know about these Vatican Children."

Arthur had backed Niccolo into a corner. "Fine."

Arthur prompted, "The Vatican Children? What are they, and how do they relate to Naomi?"

"Special children."

"You mean psychic?"

"Some of them," Niccolo said. "Others are ... something else."

"What do you mean?"

"It's impossible to explain. No, I haven't kept anything from you. I mean, it doesn't make sense."

"I've never heard of them."

"Not many people have," Niccolo said. "They remain extremely rare, and the Church keeps a list of them."

"Father Reynolds," Arthur said, scratching his chin. "In Everett. He was one of them, wasn't he?"

Niccolo nodded. "Yes. I confirmed it when I returned to the Vatican last week. His name is on the list, and they consider him one of the stronger active ones. It made one of the reasons the Church recruited him so heavily, but he had no interest in becoming an exorcist during his training."

"You can turn it down?"

"The path," Niccolo said. "Not the gift. That ... is different. The gift is incredibly rare for children to have, and rarer still for them to manifest."

"The Vatican has an interest in them? Do they kidnap them? Do they use them?"

"In the past, yes. They ... we used to gather them up and run experiments on them hundreds of years ago, but that was in the past. Now, we track them and keep our list, but no more punishment or torture. No more treating them like witches and warlocks.”

“How do you find them?”

“With difficulty, because they prove so hard to find and seem like normal children. Because of that, the Church contracts Naomi.”

“She can sense them?”

Niccolo nodded. “She has a gift and was one of the children, and is excellent for tracking down others.”

“Would Bishop Glasser know about this?”

“I don’t know,” Niccolo said. He shook his head. “I highly doubt it. It’s a closely-kept secret, known only by a handful at the Vatican. These children have such rarity that few in the Vatican even know about them. Many know about Naomi’s other exploits, however, as a thief that the Church contracts on occasion.”

“So, it’s possible the bishop hired her for another purpose? Perhaps searching for an item of value and not these children?”

“Yes. That would be my guess.”

“What, then? An artifact?”

“Possibly, but we need more information to become sure.”

Arthur hesitated. “And, that is it?”

“That is what?”

“Everything that you kept from me in the cabin? You have nothing else you want to tell me?”

“No,” Niccolo said, blinking. “God, if the Vatican knew what I had just told you ...”

“They won’t find out,” Arthur said. “But no more secrets from me, got it?”

He flipped on the car.

“Got it,” Niccolo said. “I’m sorry; I didn’t think it important.”

“*Everything* has importance, and any little detail could prove vital. I shouldn’t have to get you piss drunk just to get the truth out of you."

Niccolo nodded once, and then his eyes went wide. "Wait a second. You *wanted* me drunk?"

Arthur shrugged. "Would you have told me otherwise?"

"That's ... that's ..." Niccolo muttered in disbelief.

"*Relax*," Arthur said, as he put the car into motion. "I forgive you."

Chapter 6

After only about an hour of driving, Niccolo had fallen fast asleep in the passenger seat of Arthur's car. That sat okay with Arthur because he enjoyed the silence and solitude of the trip. It gave him time to think without interruption, and he had a lot to think about, especially where Naomi was concerned.

An old friend, though not exactly a close one, they'd known each other for years, and he'd treated with her personally on multiple occasions. She found things for the Council, and her special knack was for finding valuable Church artifacts and helping to extricate them from their owners.

He had always wondered how she managed to stay off the Church's radar after all these years. Now, he supposed he had his answer.

It stung that she would get involved in something like this. He didn't see her as a bad person, just someone who had gotten in way over her head. A criminal, yes, but Arthur had never thought of her as evil. In fact, she liked to think of herself as a modern Robin Hood and would donate huge amounts of money to charity from her conquests.

This case was different, though. Bishop Glasser had shown already that he had the willingness to summon demons and perform any manner of unspeakable acts to accomplish his mission. What did Naomi have to do with his plan?

The biggest problem was that he had no idea what the bishop's plan was. Unlike Niccolo, he didn't have the confidence that the bishop wouldn't know about the Vatican Children. An assumption like that heightened the danger, and he thought it more likely that such children were exactly what Leopold had gone after.

But, why?

It had neared three in the morning by the time they closed in on the location Elgin had given them where Naomi would hang out. Arthur had grown exhausted, and Niccolo still snored. No doubt, he would feel fairly hung over when he finally awoke.

Not that it bothered Arthur, much. Before they left the cabin, he had called ahead to ask Elgin a favor, and it had paid off. It didn't surprise Arthur that Niccolo had tried to keep something from him, and he didn't worry about it too much either. The only part of it that mattered was that he got the information in the end.

Due to his extreme tiredness, his mind grew fuzzy. They should stop and take a break for a few hours before going in after Naomi, but Arthur worried that she might know he was on the way. Elgin had promised not to warn her, but that didn't mean everyone in his crew would live up to that same promise. If Naomi knew he planned to come, she would, no doubt, set a trap for him. Or, she would warn the bishop, and they would run.

He couldn't let that happen.

Probably, she had countless traps ready anyway, just in case. A paranoid sort of person, she knew how to disappear when needed. He would have a hard time tracking her down if she got a head start.

The address Elgin had given him took them to an old water treatment facility just east of northern California that had closed down years ago. It stood too close to a fault line to maintain. Occasional earthquakes made the repair and upkeep costs of the facility astronomical. The city had long since moved their plant, abandoning this one to get reclaimed by the desert.

It offered nothing anywhere near the standard of Naomi's regular hideouts. She preferred to live in expensive apartments and high-rises surrounded by bustling cities full of well-dressed people. This abandoned water plant boasted the opposite of that.

The squat buildings appeared foreboding and grey. They encircled what looked like a graveyard of enormous pipes sticking out of the ground, and buildings that were at least a football field wide and half as long. One of the buildings had crumbled with wear, but the other three still stood. With no one maintaining them, the others would soon join the fate of the first.

He turned off the car lights and parked on a dirt road a few hundred meters outside the plant. Then he sat in the darkness and watched the building. For a good ten minutes, he waited, scanning for any signs of light or movement that would signal that someone resided here.

Nothing. No visible lights inside the complex or outside it. No patrols with flashlights or activity of any kind, but that didn't mean much in the grand scheme of things. With a complex that big, it would prove easy to hide inside one of the buildings without ever giving away your location.

Should he wake Niccolo before heading in to look for Naomi or not? On the one hand, letting the hung-over priest sleep it off while he scouted the place out seemed like a good idea, but it concerned him what might happen if Niccolo woke up to find him gone. Would he panic and come looking for him? That would make the situation much worse.

In the end, he decided to wake Niccolo. It took a few tries and a lot of shaking, but finally, the priest opened his eyes. With a groan, he rubbed his forehead.

"Wha ... what happened?"

"We've reached the site. Naomi should be somewhere inside the plant."

Niccolo perked up. "We have?"

"Yeah. Wait here. I'll come back in a couple of minutes."

Niccolo argued, "No. I'll come with you."

"It's too dangerous. Naomi likes to lay traps to catch idiots, and this could get hairy."

"Are you implying that I'm an idiot?"

Arthur shrugged. "If the shoe fits."

He smiled, hoping Niccolo knew he meant it as a joke. From the priest's expression, however, he felt unsure.

"We're in this together," Niccolo said. "I'm coming with you."

Arthur groaned internally. "No, you aren't."

"You look exhausted. *You* shouldn't go in there alone."

"It will be dangerous, and you're not ready for something like this."

"Maybe not," Niccolo said. "But I'll *not* stay behind. If even a possibility exists that Bishop Glasser is in there, then I have to go in with you. End of story."

Arthur hesitated for a moment longer. He didn't want to bring Niccolo in with him until he knew the place would bring safety or danger, but he liked the idea of having him go in as well. And, exhausted, having a fresh pair of eyes wouldn't hurt in spotting possible traps. Worse, leaving Niccolo alone could end up more dangerous. What happened if the bishop had guards patrolling the area and they stumbled across Niccolo in the car?

They would shoot before asking questions.

The safest place for Niccolo would be with Arthur. Though not ideal, it seemed better than nothing. At least by his side, Arthur could keep him safe.

Probably.

"Fine," he said. "Stay close, and don't say a word."

Niccolo nodded. "Okay."

"Do you have your tranquilizer gun?"

Niccolo held up the weapon and nodded. "Yeah."

"All right," Arthur said. "Don't shoot unless I say so."

He didn't add that he didn't want Niccolo shooting *at all* because he would likely miss. Even after the few days of training back at the cabin, he only had the confidence that Niccolo would find his target about one in every five shots. And that only if his target stood still and no outward stimuli cropped up. He had brought a lot of backup darts with them and plenty of tranquilizer, but he still didn't want to waste the ammo.

Arthur climbed out of the car, and Niccolo followed suit, closing the door behind him gently. The night air blew cool and clean this far away from the city. Arthur let it wash over him, waking him. He needed to get ready and alert in case something went down.

As they approached through the empty fields, the building grew in size. Most of the windows looked to have been knocked out by earthquakes in the preceding years. The graveyard of pipes appeared ominous on the other side of the building, though it remained completely quiet.

He made his way toward a side door of the closest building on the eastern side. Sealed up tight, it had a chain and hefty lock to keep it closed. The old door had rusted, but the chain seemed brand new. Arthur breathed easier knowing that Elgin hadn't betrayed him.

For definite, they had come to the right spot.

He dug out his lock-picking kit and knelt.

"You can pick locks?" Niccolo asked.

"Yep."

"Is this legal?"

"The city didn't put this lock here," Arthur said.

"That doesn't answer my question."

"Then, what do you think? Does breaking-and-entering sound legal?"

"Point taken."

"Keep an eye out," Arthur said. "Make sure no one sneaks up on us."

Niccolo turned around, clutching his tranquilizer gun with a shaking hand, nervous and on edge, which didn't surprise Arthur. He hadn't expected the priest to handle this easily.

He scanned the area behind and around them, squinting through the darkness to watch for anyone coming toward them. Niccolo would prove easy to sneak up on, but at least it kept him busy and out of his hair while he worked on the surprisingly complex lock.

Or, maybe, the lock was fine, and he just felt that tired.

A few moments later and it clicked free. He slipped the chain off the door and set it on the ground. Then they went inside the abandoned water treatment facility, moving through the dark interior of this building and listening for any sound of movement. Each step they took echoed in the huge chamber, though they could do little about it.

After a few minutes of searching, though, he grew confident that no one else had heard their movements. Whatever he'd expected to find in here, they found nothing. He allowed himself to relax and slipped his gun away.

With this first building producing nothing, that meant they had three left to search. Maybe, though, he would find something left behind that would show him what Naomi had gotten up to.

They moved across the first floor of the structure and discovered nothing but old and empty pipes or discarded trash. Many of the pipes had disintegrated with rust since water no longer flowed through them.

He gestured for Niccolo to stop moving, and then headed up the stairs to the second floor. The tight and grated walkway gave a clear view of the ground down below. Arthur crept along the overhanging walkways and searched for any signs that Naomi and her crew had hidden out here.

Not a thing. No traps, no signs of life. Just an empty building. A discouraging sign because it meant that maybe she had received a warning and moved along after all. If she remained here, she would have to have hidden out in one of the other adjacent structures.

Or maybe, he surmised, spotting an entrance to a basement level down below, she'd gone underground.

Alert, he headed back down to where Niccolo stood waiting and led him to an access hatch leading into the tunnels. The place would have underground maintenance access tunnels to protect some of the pipes and wiring that connected these buildings.

Without power to the building, those tunnels would

prove dark and uncomfortable and completely invisible to the outside world. They would make the perfect place for Naomi to set up shop, because even if she lit the tunnels with flood lights, nothing would be visible from the roads.

He had one flashlight with him, which he pulled out. Though he had extra ones in the car, he decided not to bother with them just now. He could test out the area, and if they found any sign of life down here, he could head back and get more gear.

"Ready?" He grabbed hold of the hatch and glanced at Niccolo.

The priest couldn't possibly have looked less ready if he had tried, but he did nod. "I guess."

"All right, then. Here goes nothing."

✳✳✳

He opened the hatch and, immediately, felt disappointed to discover nothing. No light, no sound, no anything.

Maybe he had it wrong about the tunnels providing Naomi's hiding place. For a few moments, he listened at the top of the tunnel but couldn't hear a sound.

She must have gone to ground in one of the other buildings after all. Still, it seemed worth checking the tunnels before heading to another structure.

Arthur descended the ladder into the basement, shining his flashlight back and forth. A layer of dust coated the floor, riddled with boot prints. It proved impossible to tell how fresh they were, however, considering the stillness of the area. They could be a week old, or a year.

He glanced back up at Niccolo, and then pointed at the prints, mouthing, *climb slowly*. Niccolo nodded and then came down the ladder in silence. Arthur could tell he was afraid, but he didn't complain and continued to move ahead. It impressed the Hunter, but not enough to make him confident the priest had complete control. Hopefully, the priest wouldn't panic when things turned ugly.

And knowing Naomi, things *would* turn ugly.

Arthur edged through the narrow underground tunnel, flashlight in one hand and tranquilizer gun in the other. The tunnel split off in multiple directions, following the pipes and connecting the buildings, and he followed the one with the most boot prints. That one led off to the west.

He became confident that they headed in the right direction. For once, he might manage to get the jump on Naomi rather than the other way around.

Barely had he finished the thought when a warning shout came from up ahead. It sounded like an order of some kind, but not directed at him.

"Uh oh."

A second later, the access hatch they had opened up slammed behind them, the noise echoing around them.

Definitely a trap.

"Crap."

✳✳✳

Then the shooting started. It came from further down the tunnel, ahead of them, and these people didn't have tranquilizer guns like Niccolo and himself. They fired off real lead bullets, which bounced off the tunnel walls around them.

At the same time, what sounded like a car engine revved from up ahead. It clicked and roared but didn't turn over on the first try. For a split second, a blinding light flashed at them and then went away.

A generator, he realized, but the engine had flooded, and so it hadn't started up all the way. Lucky because then the tunnel would have filled with light, and the ambushers wouldn't have to fire blindly at the two of them. The gunshots echoed through the tunnel, growing louder and drowning out all other sounds.

He stepped back and shoved Niccolo out of the way,

rounding the corner behind them and out of sight of the shooters. Niccolo tripped, and Arthur had to catch him to keep him moving, and in the process, lost his flashlight. He didn't have time to go back for it.

Luckily, it took another few cranks to start the generator, but when it flared to life, the hallway behind them became awash with bright light. The assault rifles kept firing, but Niccolo and Arthur had left their sightline.

In retreat, he pushed a terrified Niccolo back down the hallway in the direction they had come. The exit hatch had closed, so instead, he headed down another tunnel and deeper into the network. Though not ideal, their enemies had rifles, and he had sorely under-prepared for something like this.

Niccolo made gasping noises and stumbled in fear, and Arthur had to struggle to keep him moving. In the tunnel behind them, the gunshots stopped. The men had set off in pursuit. Not much time remained to get out of the way.

They made yet another turn, heading deeper into the underground complex. It grew dark again, and the floodlights had fallen out of sight. Arthur wished for his flashlight. It lay on the floor back near the ambush, and what little light reached this far in the tunnels did almost no good.

He came into a larger open area, which had a few paths leading out of it, including a short door on the right-hand side. A heavy and solid door, which hopefully led to the surface. Upon testing it, he found it unlocked, and then pushed Niccolo inside. They had to duck to get through.

On this side, the door had a pair of hefty bolts on the top and bottom. He shoved the door closed and threw both just before the pursuit team caught up to them. Angry shouts sounded on the other side, as well banging fists, but the assault had little effect on the thick metal.

A second later, the sound stopped. The attackers had, apparently, realized that the metal wouldn't yield, and no doubt, now searched for another way to get at them. Arthur glanced behind them. Two tunnels led deeper into the darkness. Which one should they take? Or ought they double back to where their attackers were?

Just now, he couldn't feel sure of much of anything.

Niccolo still gasped for air in the darkness next to him.

"What do we do?" he asked.

Arthur frowned. "I'll let you know as soon as I figure that out."

Chapter 7

While Garfield Tesfay slept off an all-nighter, his phone buzzed. If asked, he would have said he'd had a long night at work. If you asked his friends instead, they would have said a long night drinking.

Not that he had many friends.

It took him a minute to realize that something other than his alarm buzzed, and that it remained dark outside. Only one person had this number, so he knew who was calling him.

Frieda.

"You've got to be kidding me," he mumbled into his pillow, arm hanging over the side of the bed and all tingly. It had fallen asleep and felt awkward.

It took him several seconds to pull himself up from the comfortable hotel sheets, and then another minute to clear his mind enough to think straight about his situation. And during that time, Frieda's first and second call went to voicemail, and each time, Frieda was quick to dial again.

Persistent, that one.

He lay in a seedy hotel room, one of a recent string that Frieda had provided for him while on this job. He had grown used to cheap accommodations, but things had become steadily worse in the last few weeks or so. Two of his credit cards had got shut off, and the Council finance department had become nearly impossible to get hold of.

Something big had gone down, and he continued to wait for his post-mortem on what had gone wrong in the last few weeks. Maybe one of their safe houses had gotten hit, or a ranking Councilor murdered, or the Church had pulled the plug on their finances. It was hard to say exactly, but a lack of information like this just meant par for the course. He hated it but could do nothing except wait to hear.

For days, he had tried to get hold of Frieda to get an update, but so far, she'd been too busy to take or return his calls. This call would have made him happy, except that it came in the middle of the night, and he had an extreme hangover.

He snatched the cell phone off the counter and flipped it open.

"Yeah?" he muttered, clearing his throat. It tasted like he'd eaten an entire bag of cotton balls.

"I need you to get moving. You don't have a lot of time and have a lot of ground to cover."

He hadn't expected Frieda to say that at all.

"What?" he asked, still groggy. "Nothing has changed. My target has checked out for the day and won't get back on the move until the sun has set."

"This isn't about your target," Frieda said. "It's something else."

He sat up. "What *else*, Frieda? What could be more important than taking this guy down?"

"Arthur didn't check in last night. I haven't managed to get in touch with him, and I think his phone has died. He's in trouble, and you're my closest asset in the region."

He didn't think anything could piss him off faster than when Frieda called him an "asset." He nearly said something less than friendly but bit it back, and then took a deep breath. She was his boss, and if he made her mad enough, she could smother him with any number of bad jobs for the next run of months. Already, he'd fallen on her bad side and didn't want to make it any worse. "Yeah, and?"

"And," Frieda said, clearly not pleased by his response, "*you* need to get out of bed, pay the hooker, and get your ass on the road."

He ignored that middle part. Frieda just wanted to get a rise out of him. "I'm in the middle of a case. *You* put me on this case, and I've followed the target for six weeks."

"This takes priority."

"Why? Because it's Arthur?" he asked coldly.

"Because one of our own has landed in trouble," Frieda said without missing a beat. "Doesn't matter who it is; it is one of ours."

"Would you pull me off *this* case if it were anyone else?"

"Of course I would."

He wanted to call her on that and could think of multiple times she'd left him high and dry when he found himself in trouble, but his headache and hangover only helped him make bad decisions. Instead, he said, "Yeah, okay."

"We don't have time to argue," Frieda said. "Forget that it's Arthur. He's working on something critical to our organization's survival."

"So am I." Garfield sat up on his bed. "This guy has killed ten of our order in the past two years. Or did you forget?"

"It's only a few hours out of your way. You'll be gone a day or so."

"By then the trail will be cold," Garfield said. "This Wendigo won't stick around forever."

"If that happens, then we'll wait. He'll resurface, and we'll get him then."

"How long, though? Months? Years? This is the closest anyone has gotten to him in a long time, and it offers our one good chance to end him forever."

"We'll have another."

"This is a mistake."

The other end of the phone went silent for a long beat. He'd overstepped. When Frieda spoke again, her tone sounded entirely different, much colder and with an undercurrent that sent a shiver up Garfield's spine.

"I apologize if I made you think I sought your opinion," Frieda said softly. "I'm *not* asking. Get your ass on the road."

She didn't say "or else," but she also didn't need to. The threat came clear, and she felt pissed at him. She would, likely, stay angry for a while. Frieda Gotlieb could sure hold a grudge.

Before he could respond, she hung up—probably for the best. For another minute, Garfield held the phone to his ear, furious and annoyed, before flipping it closed and sliding it into his pocket. He leaned over and punched the hotel pillow, and then punched it again because of how unsatisfying it proved.

His grimy clothes felt uncomfortable and clung to him in awkward places. He couldn't smell himself, but if he could, it would be gag-worthy. When he'd returned to his hotel room, he hadn't taken a shower, and honestly, he wasn't even sure if he'd taken one this week.

Not that he much cared, though, either. His job description didn't specify that he smell good. His job bade him eliminate targets. And, apparently, to babysit the infamous Arthur Vangeest.

Garfield stood and stretched out his back. It would turn into a long day. He grabbed a bottle of whiskey from the counter. It sloshed, almost empty.

"Hair of the dog," he mumbled, taking a swig.

Though cheap and bitter swill, it would take the edge off his hangover. He would need to get breakfast soon if he planned on a long drive like this, but just now, eating sounded like a terrible idea.

Thoroughly frustrated with just about everything right now, he hated the case they'd put him on, and he hated getting pulled off it. He hated Arthur, and he hated the fact that Frieda had such power and control over him. An intimidating woman, and made considerably more so by the backing of the Council of Chaldea.

Worse still, if he pulled even a *quarter* of the crap that Arthur did on a regular basis, they would have kicked him out of the Order and executed him years ago. Hell, he thought Arthur would get executed after the stunt he pulled out in West Virginia. Going into that manor alone was a ballsy thing to do, and strictly against his orders, but all it got Arthur was a slap on the wrist.

Rules just didn't seem to apply where Vangeest was concerned.

Garfield staggered away from the bed and into the bathroom. He splashed water onto his cheeks and rubbed the stubble on his chin, and then his stomach turned, and he found himself vomiting into the cheap and dirty toilet.

Once that was over with, he felt quite a bit better, and when he finished packing up his meager belongings, he headed back out and quickly got on the road.

Maybe Frieda had it right, and his case would still be here when he got back.

Who knew, maybe pigs would even fly.

Chapter 8

"We aren't getting out that way," Arthur said to Niccolo, his voice coming from off to the left.

"Which way? If you're pointing, I can't see anything."

"The way we came in, I mean. Which means we'll have to head the other direction if we want to find another way out."

"There's another way out?"

"Definitely," Arthur said, but he didn't sound too convinced.

Suddenly, Niccolo found it difficult to swallow. He could barely see the shape of Arthur beside him in the underground tunnel, and even then, he couldn't make out his features. The air felt stale down here, and if he moved, he would bump into the walls straight away.

"Where's the flashlight?"

"Lost," Arthur said.

Too bad.

The tunnel didn't seem as dark or foreboding with the light.

Niccolo would have liked to see Arthur more clearly right about now, as well as what lay around him. Who knew, maybe he had someone other than Arthur next to him in the darkness.

He forced the thoughts away, pushing down his fear. The tunnel reminded him of the crawlspace beneath Rose's home, and the basement where Tim had confronted him in Everett. It brought back painful memories and opened fresh wounds.

"How will we know when we find another way out?" he asked, focusing on the task at hand. "We can't see anything."

The only light they did have flitted in under the doorway they had come through, and that gave only enough to make this first chamber visible. If Arthur worried at all about their predicament, he didn't show it. Instead, he dug into his pocket for his cellular flip phone.

"What are you doing?" Niccolo shook his head. "No way on Earth will you get a signal down here."

"The walls are too thick to make a call," Arthur said. "But we need more light."

As soon as the phone came on, the screen glowed like a blinding flare had set off. Though a dim screen, in fact, it still gave enough illumination to fill the room and let him see Arthur fully once more. Niccolo squinted and winced, and then reached into his pocket as well.

"No," Arthur said, holding up his hand to stop him. "Save yours. In fact, turn your phone off completely. We'll need it if we end up stuck down here for a while."

"What would you consider a while?"

Arthur didn't answer immediately. "Hours," he admitted, finally.

"Hours?" Niccolo said, incredulously.

"Maybe days. It depends on whether they want to wait us out or not."

"You said we might find a way out down those tunnels."

"We could."

"You don't sound too confident."

"Those tunnels face to the south, which means the buildings above us lay that way." He waved his hand toward the door they had come through.

"They could have access hatches."

"They could," Arthur said. "But if so, then they will likely be locked from the outside."

Niccolo's stomach sank. "So, you think we're trapped in here."

"Probably," Arthur said. "So, we should figure out where exactly *here* is."

"Two phones is all we have for light?"

Arthur nodded. "That's all we have. We need to make it count."

Arthur turned to leave and hesitated. "I'm sorry."

"For what?"

"For this," Arthur said, shaking his head. "I've gone off my game ever since ..."

Niccolo offered, "Everett?"

"It started before that, but that triggered the culmination. I feel directionless, and the old me would never have ended up in a situation like this. I'm sorry for this."

"No," Niccolo said. "Apology not accepted. You have nothing for which to apologize."

"What do you mean?"

"You might be having trouble finding your way, but that's because you're trying to find your way out of a dark place. Mistakes happen, and if we're to die down here, I would rather die because you made bad decisions trying to be a good man, than live because you made good decisions as the same man you were before."

Arthur didn't reply. Niccolo had surprised himself a little with what he said, and he found that it rang true. In the last few weeks, he had gone from hating Arthur to something akin to friendship. He surely didn't want to die down here, but if that happened, then he would accept it.

Finally, Arthur nodded at him. "We should keep moving."

"What about the door?" Niccolo asked. "We shouldn't leave it, should we?"

"It's locked, and if they try to bust it down, we will know."

"Shouldn't one of us stay here, just in case?"

Arthur didn't stop walking. "You're welcome to stay," he said over his shoulder, "but it'll get dark since you'll need to keep your phone off."

Niccolo hesitated a moment longer, groaned, and then followed Arthur down the dark tunnel.

✳✳✳

"Was this a trap? Do you think Elgin sold us out?"

"Hard to tell," Arthur said. "Definitely a trap, but I don't think he sold us out. I believe I just made a lot of mistakes, but Naomi is also good at her job. We just set off their defenses, and they responded. Naomi has a reputation for paranoia, but if she'd known we were coming, I don't think she would try to kill us. I reckon she would run."

"You sure about that?"

Arthur hesitated longer than Niccolo would have liked, and when he finally answered, it didn't sound convincing. "Yeah, I'm sure."

"What do we do now?"

"Now, we try to find a way out of here. Even if the access hatches lock from up above, there is a chance one of them has rusted enough that we can break it open."

"What happens if we can't, and we get stuck down here?"

Arthur frowned. "Then we will have to try plan B."

"What's plan B?"

"We don't have one yet."

✳✳✳

They walked through the pitch-black tunnels in silence, Arthur up in front, and Niccolo keeping an eye behind. Arthur had turned the screen light as dim as possible, but already, the battery ran near empty. Niccolo couldn't even feel certain when he'd last charged his phone, and it would surprise him if it hadn't fallen under halfway by the time he'd turned it off.

He held the tranquilizer gun Arthur had given him in his hand, clutching it for dear life, and couldn't imagine letting it go. When Arthur had trained him how to use it, the lessons had seemed pointless and exhausting, but now he wished he'd paid more attention.

Niccolo breathed as quietly as he could, but each inhalation sounded like a hurricane in the echoing quiet of the tunnels. Occasionally, something else bounced back to them, most likely coming from outside their locked doorway, but he couldn't tell for sure.

It worried him that in his fear, he might also imagine phantom sounds around them. Soft noises came like a dripping sound from somewhere around them. It proved difficult to tell what had reality and what only happened in his head.

He focused solely on following Arthur and watching the hallway behind him, and he tried not to imagine what horrible things might lurk just out of sight.

They ran into dead-end after dead-end with all the access hatches locked and bolted from the other side. Enormous rusty pipes wound along the walls in groups, and at various intersections, went through the ceiling and to the sky above. Once in a while, the tunnel became so narrow that it forced him to suck in his ample gut to get through.

After about an hour, and just when his claustrophobia had nearly got the best of him, the cellphone Arthur carried lost power. It flickered, and Niccolo's heart jumped into his throat.

"Damn," Arthur muttered.

They managed to keep moving for another few minutes before the light went out altogether.

"Your turn," Arthur said.

He didn't need to say it, though. Already, Niccolo had reached for his pocket. They stood in the heavy darkness for a moment while Niccolo fished out his phone. He flipped it open and held the power button until it turned on. It lit up the area in front of them.

Though dim, in the utter darkness it felt bright. Quickly, he lowered the brightness to the lowest setting, and then handed it over to Arthur. The Hunter put his phone away and set off walking once more down the tunnel. They reached another tight section of pipes and squeezed through.

"You skipped an access hatch back there," Niccolo said after a minute

"Did I?" Arthur asked. "Probably locked."

"What if it wasn't?"

"It probably was."

Niccolo didn't like that answer. In their current state, he felt that everything should get checked. "We should try them *all*."

Arthur hesitated. "We need to keep moving."

"But—"

"Let's just keep moving," Arthur said. "Stay close behind me."

Niccolo wanted to object but changed his mind. Arthur knew best in a situation like this, and he had to admit that he had jumped in way over his head. They continued walking, Niccolo still keeping an eye behind them.

"How big is this place?" Niccolo asked, finally.

"Big," Arthur said.

"But, I mean, *how* big? We've walked for what feels like hours."

"Why do you ask? Are you getting tired?"

"I felt tired a while ago. Now I feel exhausted."

"That's good."

"What?"

"Never mind."

Arthur fell silent. They walked for a few more moments before Niccolo spoke up again.

"What did you mean? Why is it *good* that I'm exhausted?"

"No reason."

"No, tell me. What did you mean to say?"

Arthur sighed and stopped walking. "This place isn't that big at all."

"What?" Niccolo asked, incredulous. "But we've been walking for *hours*."

Arthur stared at him. "In a circle."

Niccolo stared back. "A what?"

"A circle. Not a big one, either. We've checked the same three access hatches, like, sixty times."

"You mean you've led us *in circles*?"

"That's what I said, yes."

"Why?"

"To keep moving."

"How long have you known?"

"Since the first time we made the loop," he said. "I wanted to suggest we just keep walking to occupy ourselves. Tiredness helps combat fear. I figured I would just suggest it when you bought it up, but ... well ..."

It dawned on Niccolo. "That's why you ignored those access hatches."

"I grew tired of checking each one time and again. At first, it seemed funny, but now it's just draining."

It made so much sense now that Arthur had said it aloud. The fact that they had turned slightly to the left constantly, the tight section of pipes ...

"Oh," he said.

Arthur didn't respond. He turned around and just kept walking down the hallway. Niccolo stood there for a long moment before rushing to follow him.

"You mean for these last three hours you've made me *think* we had headed *deeper* into this place and might find a way out?"

"Four hours, actually. And, no, I didn't *make* you do anything," Arthur said. "It seemed cruel to disenfranchise. Each hatch we got to, you grew so hopeful that it would let us out."

"So, we won't get out of here?"

"Nope," Arthur said. "Not through these hatches, at least. Our only way out is via the door we came in through."

"We can bust our way out?"

"I'm good. But not that good."

"What, then?"

"We wait," Arthur said. "And, we walk—walking helps me think, and it keeps you from falling to the ground and crying. Trust me; the darkness would get to you after a while. The last thing I wanted you to do is sit in the dark with your thoughts."

Niccolo stopped walking, shocked, and then burst out laughing.

"What's so funny?"

"Everything," Niccolo said. "This. All of this. It's just funny."

"There are a lot of words I would use to describe this, and funny doesn't even make the list."

"I mean, you and me trapped in this tunnel in the middle of the desert with no way out. I would *never* have thought I would die like this."

"It isn't how we'll die," Arthur said. Then, he added, "Not me, at least."

"Really? I don't see any way out of this, so if you do, maybe you should enlighten me before I go out of my mind."

"Right now, my best plan is to wait for help."

"Help from who?"

"Frieda," Arthur said. "I am more than a few hours late on a check-in, so she knows we've landed in trouble. I also told her where we would head, so she has the location."

"Why didn't you say that earlier?"

"Because it's my hope, but it might not prove true."

"What?"

"I miss check-ins all the time, and it might take a couple of days for her realize something has, in fact, gone wrong."

"*A couple of days*?" Niccolo said at a near-shout.

"That's a *small* possibility."

"How do you miss check-ins? That's the entire point of a check-in. To check ... in."

"Sometimes I get busy," Arthur said. "This job isn't exactly on a normal schedule."

The fear bubbled up inside Niccolo once more.

"So, we get trapped in this tunnel, and now you tell me we have no way out, armed people wait on the other side of that door who plan to kill us, and the only person who knows we're down here *might* send someone to rescue us?"

"Basically."

"No wonder you just kept walking."

"We might have another option," Arthur said. "We could always try to negotiate."

"With Bishop Glasser?" Niccolo shook his head violently. "I would rather just die down here with you."

"Then, let's try to relax. We'll run out of light soon, and then we won't be able to walk anymore. We can find somewhere to hole up near the door and just wait it out. If help is on the way, then it should get here in only a short while."

"And, if it isn't?"

Arthur hesitated. "Then it will be a long next couple of days."

Chapter 9

Garfield called Frieda to get directions once he had left his hotel, but he hung up as soon as she had given an address. Although she would expect regular updates, he didn't want to talk to her until he'd made it to Arthur. The sun came up, and he felt better, but he still needed more sleep.

He doubted he would get any; at least, not anytime soon. It would take a four-hour drive to get to the water treatment plant to which Frieda had sent him, and he couldn't help but feel curious about what Arthur had gotten himself into.

He needed more information about what he had to deal with. Not a lot of traffic met him while he drove through the empty deserts, and even though it had reached early in the afternoon and the sun lay behind him, he wore his shades. Most likely, dusk would fall at around six at this time of year, and maybe earlier.

After a few hours driving, while on the freeway heading west, he called Frieda again. "Where am I going?" He flipped open his map of Arizona on the passenger seat and glanced down at it.

To see the paper better, he snapped his shades up, and then took another sip of his Styrofoam coffee. He had picked it up when he got gas, along with a hotdog that had probably been spinning for a week. It had tasted disgusting and half-rotten, but he'd managed to choke it down. He liked to think he had an iron stomach.

When not drinking, that was.

"I gave you the address."

"That address points to the middle of nowhere. I don't think it will help me find Arthur."

"It's a big facility. Might not be on the maps, but it's out there. I'm sure you can't miss it."

"What should I expect to find?"

"Arthur," she said, as if the answer were obvious.

"I mean aside from Arthur. Do you know what he was

doing or working on?"

As much as he didn't like Arthur, the guy was effective and wouldn't likely get himself into trouble. Whatever proved too much for him to handle, gave enough to keep Garfield on his toes.

"I don't know."

"You sent him out there."

"I didn't," Frieda said. "Not exactly. He's following up leads, and this was his best one."

"What job is he on?"

No answer.

"Frieda ... I can't help if you won't tell me what's going on."

The other end of the line stayed silent for a long moment. Would she even give him an answer? Finally, she spoke again.

"He's hunting a bishop."

"A *what?*"

"Bishop Leopold Glasser," Frieda said. "He's summoned demons and murdered countless people."

"You're kidding, right?"

"I wish."

"Then, Arthur's on Church business? Why haven't we called them for help?"

"It goes deep," Frieda said. "We can't involve the Church until we know if the bishop is working with anyone."

"Was that your call, or Arthur's?"

"Mine," she said, though not without a slight hesitation.

Garfield hadn't known how things could get any crazier in this rescue mission, but there it was. The Council had a fickle relationship with the Church at the best of times, and they rarely got asked to help them on such critical Church business as hunting down a wayward bishop.

"Does he have permission from the Church?"

"He's working with an exorcist investigating this issue."

Not a proper answer, but Garfield knew better than to press the issue. The thing was, if Arthur had done something like this *without* the Church's permission …

Then they all trod on thin ice.

"Sure," he said. "Then, I guess I better get there sooner rather than later."

"That would be best."

"You said it's a huge facility?"

"Water treatment plant. Just head to that location I gave you, and you'll find it with no trouble. How far out do you think you are?"

He glanced at the paper a couple of times and ran some quick math in his head. "About five more hours," he said. "Give or take. I'll get there by sundown."

"Drive faster."

"You want me to get pulled over? I've got enough firepower in the trunk to go after Fort Knox."

"Just get there."

"I will," he said. "Should I know anything else? Should I expect to find this wayward bishop at the treatment plant?"

"I don't know. But Arthur went looking for Naomi."

"Naomi Develon?" Garfield rubbed his chin and chuckled. "No wonder he got himself into trouble."

Naomi had gained notoriety for extreme paranoia. Garfield hated her and refused to work with her because she acted so stuck up and arrogant. She always over-prepared for any situation and broke rules any chance she got.

"Is she a target?"

"No," Frieda said. "Not yet, at least. Right now, Arthur has only gone after Bishop Glasser. He wanted to find Naomi for information, I think."

"Why do I know that name?" He wracked his brain. "Bishop Glasser. You keep saying it, and I feel like I've heard it before."

"He's related to Emily," Frieda said. "Cousins."

"Oh, yeah," he said. Then it hit him. "Shit. Then that means …"

"I told you that this was critical to the Council's survival. There's a reason we need this dealt with ASAP."

"Jesus, Frieda," Garfield mumbled. "Could things get any worse?"

"The bishop helped murder Arthur's family," Frieda said.

Garfield coughed. "I meant that as a joke."

He remembered those first weeks after Arthur's family got murdered, and the ripple effect it had sent through their Order. They had all felt terrified after that, suddenly feeling vulnerable in ways they had never dreamed possible.

Garfield didn't have any kids, but he did have siblings and a nephew named Dominick. If someone had murdered his family the way they had Arthur's, he didn't know what he would have done.

Probably something similar to what Arthur actually did do, come to think of it. Anyone he thought might be tangentially responsible for their deaths would lay rotting in the ground right about now.

"Now, you know everything I know," she said. "See what happened to Arthur and the priest. Everything hinges on this mission. Whatever the bishop plans, it will prove as bad for us as it will for the Church. We need a win, Garfield. Don't let me down."

"You think Arthur is down?"

"I don't think anything yet," Frieda said. "That's why I'm sending you."

"What if *I* need backup?"

For something like this, it seemed odd that Frieda would have come to him for help. Normally, she would have flown in multiple assets to deal with a threat this large. Especially for Arthur. She knew that the two of them didn't get along that well, and no doubt, she had to worry that Garfield wouldn't feel willing to put in a lot of effort to save him.

So, why hadn't she sent in more help?

"What haven't you told me?" he asked. "Why am I the only one you've sent for something this big?"

"We can't spare the extra resources."

"Why not?"

Silence on the other end of the line. Finally, she said, "Just call me when you know something."

Without giving him a chance to respond, she hung up again, a habit of hers that grated on his nerves. She always liked to have the last word in any conversation.

Garfield thought over what Frieda had admitted to him and realized that things might turn out even more dangerous than she had let on. If the Church had involvement with something like this all the way up to the level of a bishop, then it would spell years of fallout.

Something else Frieda had said clicked for him—he'd heard rumors that Emily Glasser had fallen out of favor with the Council and that they would hold a trial for her sometime in the future, but he had thought those just rumors. The idea that her family had become involved with something like this ...

Still, it didn't concern him overly much. Not his problem. If things went wrong, it could spell disaster for Frieda and the Council, but it wouldn't affect him. With his talents, he could always find more work.

He cranked up the music, rolled down the windows, and cruised on down the road.

Chapter 10

"How long have we been down here?"

"Too long." Arthur leaned back against the wall and let out a sigh. The batteries in both phones had long since gone dead, and he felt exhausted. A while earlier, he had taken a short nap, but it hadn't lasted long before Niccolo woke him. Niccolo's fear had intensified, and the longer they stayed trapped down here, the worse it would get.

Anyway, being in the pitch-black confines of the tunnel and tasting the stale air didn't make it easy to sleep. On the contrary, their situation kept his nerves on edge and wouldn't allow him to relax.

"Control your breathing," Arthur said. "If you let in the fear, you'll start gasping. If that happens, you'll hyperventilate. And then you'll end up passing out."

"I don't want to fall unconscious."

"That's why you have to control your breathing," Arthur said. "Focus only on taking breaths in and out. Let the rest of the world slip away."

He listened to Niccolo's breathing. It sounded calm for a few breaths, but then came the rapid-fire inhalations once more, which told Arthur it was a lost cause. The only way to help Niccolo deal with his mounting panic would be to get him out of these access tunnels.

An occasional noise still sounded from outside the door in the hallway, which made it clear their assailants remained out there. At the beginning of this misadventure, he had expected them to try and speak to him through the doorway, but only silence came from the other side.

Not encouraging. Naomi wasn't a killer, and he expected her to try and open a line of communication. Once she found out that they had Arthur trapped, he had hoped to try and negotiate his way out of this situation.

If she didn't feel in the negotiating mood—or, worse, if she wasn't even the one out there—then things would just get worse for the two of them. From everything he knew about Bishop Glasser, Arthur didn't like their odds of getting any mercy.

Pissed at himself for getting stuck in this situation at all, he hadn't grown quite ready to blame it on his desire not to kill people anymore. Even if he had his revolver with him, he would still have made the same decisions that got them trapped here. After all, the men in the hallway carried assault rifles and stood ready for war.

It still ate away at him, though. In his line of work, hesitation meant death. He might have just gotten the two of them killed because of his newfound inability to do whatever proved necessary to accomplish his mission.

More than all of that, though, he now worried that Frieda hadn't sent anyone to come rescue them. A long time had passed, and nothing had changed. Maybe she had sent someone, and they had been unsuccessful. Or, maybe she didn't know they had gone missing at all. A pretty good chance existed that no help would come, but he didn't want to let Niccolo know that.

Niccolo barely hung on as it was. The silence and darkness had crept under his skin, and he teetered on the verge of a complete meltdown. The priest wouldn't last much longer.

"Do you think our air is running out?" the priest asked, suddenly, his voice splitting the silence. Niccolo panted on the other side of the tunnel. Arthur could imagine the terrified man tugging at his collar.

"No," Arthur said. "The *tunnel* has ventilation."

"Are you sure? I mean, it feels like the air has grown thinner. I feel ... I feel like I can't breathe."

"Calm down," Arthur said. "You're fine. It's all in your mind. Just try to relax."

"How the hell am I supposed to relax at a time like this?"

"Deep breaths."

Niccolo didn't speak for a few more minutes. Then he

said, "Do you think it's daytime now?"

Arthur estimated, "Mid-afternoon." After a pause, he said, "Maybe closer to evening. We've been trapped in here for about twelve hours."

"Twelve hours? No wonder I feel starved."

"It's water we need. Not food."

"That too. Has it really been that long?"

"At least," Arthur said. "If not longer."

On the other side of the room, Niccolo stood and paced. He scuffed his feet and ran his hands along the walls, and gradually, his breathing accelerated.

Arthur rubbed his face and sighed. "Come on, Niccolo. Try to relax. This isn't helping."

"It's helping *me*."

"No, it isn't. You need to get in control of your emotions and fear. Focus on your breathing and on relaxing. No one has ever gotten more mastery over themselves by letting their emotions run wild."

"I don't want mastery over myself. I want to get out of *here*."

"Sit down and think about something else."

"Like what?"

"I don't know," Arthur said. He needed to keep Niccolo talking about other things to distract him from the worry. "Why did you decide to come out here with me? I hadn't expected that back in Everett."

"Because the bishop needs to get stopped."

"He will," Arthur said. "Whether or not you help me, I'll take him down. That doesn't explain why *you* came out here, though. You haven't trained for something like this."

"I'm an exorcist."

"Demons don't use assault rifles," Arthur said. Then he shrugged. "Usually."

"It's still my job to protect people."

"It's your job to *help* people. You can't help them if you're dead, so why put yourself at risk for something like this? Why not let the professionals deal with it?"

Niccolo fell silent for a long minute. Arthur didn't know if he stood pondering his answer or panicking, but finally, he spoke once more.

"I've wondered the same thing, myself. I guess ... I just wanted to help. My entire life, I didn't believe things like this had any reality. I became an exorcist who never believed in demons. I felt like, with all this craziness in the world, I couldn't just sit back and let it be someone else's problem."

"Fair enough."

"Why do you do it?"

"I just always have," Arthur said. "It's a part of my life."

"That doesn't make sense. You mean you did this as a kid?"

"I mean as far back as I can remember," Arthur said. "And, yes, I started training at about fourteen years old. I never had an alternative path."

"What would you have done if you didn't do this?"

Arthur didn't have a good answer. He'd never stopped to consider how his life might have unfolded if he'd never become a Hunter for the Council.

"I don't know," Arthur said, after a pause. "My brother, Mitchell, is my only real family, and he got me involved in this life when I was still in middle school. I never even considered another career. Plus, I became good at it."

"That isn't a proper answer."

"No, I suppose not. I guess if I had another option, I would most likely have joined the Church."

"Become a priest?"

"Yes," Arthur said. "I always wanted to be a Reverend. Reverend Arthur Vangeest."

"You still can."

"No. The Church would never accept me. Not with what I've done."

This time, Niccolo said nothing, which didn't surprise Arthur. He took the man's silence as assent with his assessment. After all, only a few weeks ago, Niccolo had considered Arthur to be a mass murderer and a danger to society. Truth was, Niccolo had it right. He doubted if Niccolo considered him worthy of the Lord's forgiveness.

"Just relax," he said into the silence. "Try to keep your mind occupied with other thoughts and don't worry about what waits outside that door. Someone will come to rescue us."

"Really?"

Arthur lied, "Definitely. For sure, help is on its way as we speak."

Chapter 11

It didn't take long for Garfield to locate Arthur's rental car outside the water treatment facility to which Frieda had sent him. As she had said, the buildings proved impossible to miss out in the middle of nowhere. It looked like they had been set up with the intention of forming a town around them and then simply become abandoned.

The car sat parked off a dirt road only a short ways west of the facility, and easy to spot since he knew for what he should search. Naomi and her crew would also have found it easy to spot, though. And seeing it out in the open like that only further annoyed Garfield. Arthur tended toward carelessness and always seemed in a hurry, and it put him in bad situations all the time.

It stemmed to the root of his personality. The man always rushed and made mistakes. Arthur would never have walked into that occult den in West Virginia if not so rash and impatient, and one day, that attitude would get him killed.

Maybe today was that day.

Garfield, on the other hand, would have taken the time to find a better place to stow his car or keep it further away from the treatment plant. Most of their job dictated staying one step ahead of the enemy, and he took that seriously. Any patrols of the area would have had little trouble spotting this and giving away Arthur's incursion, and it had cost Arthur the chance to end the Wendigo once and for all.

Now, Garfield had to clean up Arthur's mess. It sickened him because Arthur had been elevated to the status of a legendary Hunter after what he'd pulled in West Virginia. The shining example of what their Order *could* achieve, and yet here he had ended up, trapped in a water treatment plant by a seedy underworld dealer and a wayward bishop, of all people.

Some legend he had turned out to be.

Garfield suppressed the thoughts. Part of his dislike for

Arthur stemmed from jealousy, though he would never have admitted as much aloud.

He pulled off the road and into the woods behind Arthur's car—much farther out of sight—and parked. Then, he circled to his trunk. He popped it open and surveyed his collection of guns, explosives, and other death-dealing instruments. Enough firepower lay in there to match any survivalist's wet dream.

Garfield had something for all occasions, depending on what sort of situation/monster he had to deal with. He liked to prepare for any occurrences.

For now, he grabbed a pair of pistols, a sawed-off shotgun, and a couple of knives. From Frieda's estimation of the situation, it sounded like Arthur had gotten himself caught by plain old humans, which seemed even more embarrassing than something supernatural.

He closed the trunk, covered the car in branches and leaves to camouflage it a little, and then began the cautious trek toward the closest treatment facility building. Arthur would have gone there, he figured.

It was a fairly open and hilly area just outside of California, which meant that mostly empty terrain and wooded areas surrounded him. Nothing lurked nearby to offer solid cover, so he became entirely exposed as he made his way forward. However, he didn't see anyone in the vicinity. That meant little, though, because an enemy could have stood a mile off with binoculars in just about any direction and watched his approach. At least the sun had set, and he didn't have to walk in broad daylight.

He kept his eyes peeled for any signs of movement, but the entire place remained quiet. No one showed up to stop him, nor did any alarms get set off. Had Frieda led him wrong? Might he have come to the wrong place?

When he reached the door, however, he knew he was on the right path. A huge chain lay discarded on the ground nearby, and it looked new. Someone had come this way recently, and something lay inside that they wanted to hide.

One final time, he checked his weapons to make sure everything remained in working order. Satisfied, he pushed the door open and went inside.

✳✳✳

Extreme dark and quiet met him inside the huge and sprawling facility. He waited just inside the doorway for a moment, listening for any sounds and giving his eyes time to adjust to the dimness. A smudge of light filtered in overhead from high windows, but not enough to pierce the black.

No sounds reached him at all. It brought a heavy and pervasive silence. If Naomi hid at this plant, then she definitely didn't occupy this building.

What would Naomi do with Arthur? That question had nagged at Garfield since he set off on the drive out here. Naomi hadn't exactly become one of Garfield's favorite people, but she also didn't stand among his enemies, either. She worked for the Council—at least, she used to.

If she held Arthur hostage, or if she had killed him, then she had crossed a lot of lines that she might not cross back from easily. If that were the case, then Garfield might have no choice except to kill her.

Satisfied his eyes had adjusted as much as they could, Garfield moved forward into the dark building. Though he had a flashlight, he didn't want to use it and give away his position. He had trained to work in situations like this, and unless his enemy had night-vision goggles, he felt satisfied he could maintain the upper hand.

With his breathing controlled, he moved across the cement flooring, using a light tread to make as little noise as possible, and listening and watching for any sign that someone else lurked nearby. This old complex had several buildings, and Arthur could be in any one of them, so the further he could get in his exploration without Naomi or the bishop knowing of his presence, the better.

He had almost completely cleared the upper floor of this building when he heard movement from down below him. On the second-floor railing, he slid out of sight, held the shotgun ready at his side, and waited.

A few seconds later, footsteps clacked against a metal ladder. Then came more shuffling and a grunt as someone climbed out of a hatch in the flooring, and then a flashlight beam lit up the area.

The beep of a walkie-talkie chimed.

"It's clear," a man's voice said as the flashlight beam continued its sweep. Garfield heard the muffled sound of someone talking on the other end of the line, but he couldn't make out any of the words. "Probably just a rabbit or something tripping a sensor. Those things are way too sensitive."

More murmuring on the other end.

"Yeah, I know. I'll sweep the perimeter. Back in ten."

The flashlight continued to wave when the guard headed toward to the doorway leading outside. He went to the opposite door that Garfield had come in through. The Hunter kept perfectly still until he heard the door open and then close once more, and then he crept out of his hiding place.

"Guess I came to the right place," Garfield muttered, turning back toward the hatch that the guard had come up through. He had an idea of where he might find Arthur and Naomi.

***

Garfield moved silently through the manmade underground tunnel beneath the facility, following the pipes deeper into the complex. He held his shotgun with one hand and ran his other along the wall to keep his bearings in the near absence of light.

Though he couldn't see anything, he trusted his other senses to alert him of any danger in the area ahead. The man he'd seen up above had carried a flashlight instead of wearing goggles, which meant Garfield could still use the darkness to his advantage.

Occasionally, a sound echoed from the tunnels ahead of him—a murmured voice bouncing off the walls—and he used it to guide him in the correct direction. Gradually, the words grew in volume and clarity until he came near enough to their source that he could see their light.

"This is taking too long," a man said. He sounded in his mid-to-late fifties and gruff. "We should go in there and get them."

"They have no way out," a woman said. He recognized it as Naomi's voice. "The tunnels remain locked down on their side. I'll not risk any of my men on a suicide mission. They have no food or water, so we can just wait it out and, eventually, they will surrender and come out."

"So you've said."

"It would make it easier to get them to surrender if we talked to them. We can see who's come and figure out what they want. Maybe we can strike a deal and send them on their way."

"No. It doesn't matter who they are; they came here for *me*. They need to die."

Naomi made a sucking sound with her teeth, something she did when displeased with a response. "Fine. But, if we won't talk to them, we'll do this *my* way."

"I'm paying you a fortune to handle this situation."

"Not enough to risk lives when not necessary. They've been in there for a long time, and it won't take long until they beg us to let them out. A while longer and they'll feel ready to do anything we tell them."

The two speakers stood around the corner, about twenty feet ahead of Garfield, though he doubted the two talkers had come alone. The sound of movement made him think that at least five or six people waited up ahead, and maybe more.

The man Naomi spoke to was probably the bishop,

Garfield realized. He assumed they talked about Arthur, and somehow, they'd managed to force him into a locked area of some sort. From the sounds of it, he'd been stuck in there for quite a while, too.

Hopefully not too long that Arthur wouldn't be any help, though. A lot of guys stood up ahead, armed to the teeth. And knowing Naomi, those guards would prove well trained. If this were to be a successful rescue mission, then he would need Arthur's help.

Soft shoes paced across the floor.

"We don't have time for this," the bishop said, after a moment. "I need to get back to my children."

"I told you to go."

"And leave you here alone? So you can let them escape?"

"I won't. You have my word."

He laughed sardonically. "What value is your word?"

"If you don't trust me, then why have me here?"

"Remember who is in charge."

"I know full well how important all of this is to you."

"I can't leave and run the risk of them getting out and trailing me. Leave your men here to take care of it. If you come with me, I have confidence in their loyalty."

A suitable suggestion, Garfield reckoned. It would make his job *a lot* easier.

"No," Naomi said, though her voice sounded less confident now. "I'm not in the habit of abandoning things halfway. It won't take long now. Once they get desperate enough, they will either turn themselves in or try to force past us. And then we can leave."

After Naomi finished speaking, the two of them fell silent. Garfield listened for movement, and then decided that closer to five people stood up ahead. Also, a few would have gone out on patrol or would guard other exits, which meant maybe upwards of seven armed soldiers in total.

Not great odds.

Garfield steadied his breathing and peeked around the

corner. A spotlight aimed at a closed doorway gave them their light source. No doubt Arthur had become trapped behind there, which explained why he hadn't checked in with Frieda.

Six people, Garfield counted. Four guards in positions facing toward the closed door, as well as Naomi and the bishop. Naomi's mercenaries had huddled behind boxes and crates to give them cover; though, at this point, three of them had sat down. They had waited here for a long time, and the boredom had got to them.

Naomi looked disheveled and tired as she sat on one of the pipes. The other man, Garfield didn't recognize, and he took him to be the bishop. This older man wore robes and had a priest's collar around his neck. With his shaved head, he seemed decidedly unpleasant to look at.

Had he been the one speaking? The speaker had mentioned children in his conversation with Naomi and that he needed to get back to them, which didn't make sense. Bishops weren't allowed to marry or have families unless they left the Church. Maybe it was someone else.

Naomi, a woman in her early-forties, appeared fit but with a few extra pounds tacked on. Pretty and charismatic, she had a round face and almond-colored eyes.

The priest frowned as he studied Naomi. His eyes narrowed, and his look changed to one considerably darker.

"You know who it is in there, don't you?"

When he spoke, Garfield recognized the voice as that which had talked to Naomi earlier.

What children?

"What?" she asked, taking a guarded step away from him.

"You're manipulating me," the man said. "You *know* who is trapped in there, and you don't want to go in and kill him. Do you?"

"What are you *talking* about?" Naomi asked. "Of course I don't know who it is. How would I know?"

Though she made a convincing liar, Garfield had known

her long enough to tell when she wasn't being honest. This became one of those times.

Apparently, the bishop could tell too.

"You're ready to end our alliance, then?"

A moment passed. Naomi's expression changed when she realized he wouldn't believe her any longer.

"What alliance?" she asked, an edge of anger in her voice. "You didn't give me a lot of options in the situation, did you?"

"I paid you handsomely."

"I never wanted your damned money," she said with venom in her tone. "And I sure as hell won't kill Arthur Vangeest and whoever came with him. I don't want *that* blood on my hands."

The bishop studied her for a moment, and then nodded.

"Very well. Then, I must kill you too."

"Is that right? Quite a feat, considering we outnumber you five to one. These are my men, after all. Or, did you forget?"

"Oh?" he said. "Are they your men? It must have slipped my mind."

Suddenly, three of the guards swiveled their guns toward the fourth. That unlucky man still stood watching the doorway, oblivious to the drama. The tunnels filled with the concussive blasts of gunshots when those three opened fire on him.

He tried to respond and bring his gun to bear but too late. They caught him off-guard and unprepared.

The poor guy staggered back into the wall, and his gun fell to the ground. Slowly, he slid to the floor, leaving a trail of blood from multiple wounds along the tunnel above him.

Naomi reacted quickly, reaching for a gun strapped to her hip, but before she could draw it, all three guards swung back to put her in their crosshairs. She stopped moving, and ever so slowly, took her hand off the grip of her pistol.

"Your *men*," the bishop said, smiling at her. "My demons."

"Bastard," she said, barely above a whisper.

"People have called me a lot of things in my life. One of them is overly cautious. A great many people warned me about you, and that when the time came, you wouldn't feel willing to do the necessary."

"You've planned this since the beginning."

"Prepared, yes. Planned, no. Your talents offered far too much value for me to want to scrub you out of existence like this. I had hoped the rumors would prove wrong. I hoped I wouldn't have to kill you."

"Not much choice now, huh?"

His smile grew even wider. "My dear, we *always* have a choice." He turned to face the three possessed guards. "Tie her up and kill Arthur and his friend. Don't hurt her, though. We will need the vessel in perfect condition when we take her to Jeremy."

Naomi's eyes widened, and Garfield guessed what would happen next. He had no clue who Jeremy was, or what the bishop meant, but something would go down imminently. No way in hell would Naomi let them take her alive to become a vessel for some demon.

Once more, she reached for her gun. That gave Garfield his cue to act. He took a deep breath, stepped around the corner, and readied his shotgun.

The closest guard stood only ten feet away, and he remained wholly focused on Naomi, who stood in front of him. He didn't even have the slightest clue that someone occupied the hallway behind him until Garfield spoke.

"*Hey, dumbass,*" Garfield hollered, aiming his shotgun.

The guy glanced over his shoulder, a look of shock on his face. He swung his gun around, but entirely too slowly.

Garfield pulled the trigger, and buckshot hit the man right in the chest. It threw him backward, toward his friends like he'd gotten hit with a sledgehammer. He slammed into the pipes running along the wall and tumbled sideways, landing in a heap behind them.

The rifles had sounded loud, but this seemed like a jet-engine had mated with a stick of dynamite in the tunnel. It roared painfully in the narrow space for a few long seconds before, finally, dissipating and leaving his ears ringing.

Garfield didn't wait, pumping another round into the chamber and aiming at the second guard. This one proved faster on the reaction, diving to the side to get cover behind some crates. He moved fast and with super-human agility. A demon.

Garfield fired anyway, but couldn't be sure if he managed to clip the demon in the leg, or if his shot had missed completely.

The other guard ignored the distraction and fired at Naomi, but she had moved as soon as Garfield had shown up in the hall. She ripped her gun free and ran toward nearby boxes, firing blindly at the guard as she went for cover.

A shot clipped her, and she stumbled, but then she managed to return a clear shot of her own. That bullet landed, but if the demon even noticed the wound, it didn't let on.

Garfield moved forward, chambering another round, but by now, the other guard hiding behind the box had recovered from the initial engagement. He fired a hail of bullets from his assault rifle, forcing Garfield to rush back and duck around the corner once more.

Garfield waited until the rifle ran dry, and then leaned back around the corner. Naomi lay on the ground, though he couldn't tell if she had died or just lay injured. The guard that had shot at her turned around to face him, and the other one that had fired at him now reloaded another clip.

"*Sayanora, sucker,*" Garfield shouted, aiming his shotgun at that guard and pulling the trigger.

It clicked.

A misfire.

He tried to pump it, but the unfired shell jammed inside the action and locked it up.

Garfield stared at it with a feeling of utter betrayal. "I

meant to clean it," he murmured.

When he looked up, the possessed mercenaries came toward him. The closer one had almost finished loading another clip into his rifle. His eyes looked blank, and he grinned as he came toward Garfield.

Not enough time to draw his pistol against both of them. Garfield cursed, turned, and ran back down the hallway from whence he'd come. They fired at him, but he got out of their line of sight, and the shots hit the wall behind him.

The shooting stopped, and the bishop shouted at the two remaining guards, "You! After him. You, stay here."

Garfield ignored them all and kept running, heading back toward the next level and higher ground. Along the way, he drew his pistol, hoping like hell that it would serve him better than the shotgun had.

If not, then he would end up in a world of hurt, and his only chance lay in him relying on Arthur to come to his aid. He didn't have to worry whether or not Arthur had heard the gunshots, though.

"Pretty sure he knows I'm here."

✱✱✱

The sound of the weapons would have proved impossible to miss even if the door had twice its thickness. Arthur sat up, hearing blasts echo from outside the door. The metal muted the sound, but it remained distinctive. One, in particular, sounded extremely loud, and Arthur guessed that it came from a shotgun.

"What was that?" Niccolo leaned forward, little more than a shape in the darkness, and Arthur could practically feel the priest's discomfort at the situation.

"That," Arthur said, "gives us our signal that the time has come to leave."

"Frieda?"

"Maybe, but we can't know for sure. Either way, we

need to move *now*."

Arthur stood, sliding his dart gun out of his belt. Part of him—a large part, if he were honest—wished he had something heftier with him when he opened that door. It seemed like one thing to train with a weapon like this and theorize its usefulness, but something entirely different to stand in this situation and only have a measly tranquilizer to defend him.

These non-lethal guns felt too light and flimsy for his taste, and the fact that he only had three shots would make a huge test of his patience. It made him feel naked and weak, something he had definitely not grown used to.

He needed more shots, at least.

"Your gun," Arthur said. "Give it to me."

He reached out and grabbed Niccolo by the shoulder. A second later, he felt the second gun pressed into his hand.

"Here."

"All right. Stay behind me."

"No problem."

More gunshots came from outside, though Arthur found it impossible to tell how far away or how many people had fired. The twisted and imaginative part of his mind could imagine the guards standing out there, firing off shots to draw him out. It could mean a trap or a distraction.

He didn't have time to worry about that, though. If they had laid a trap, then he would walk right into it, but if he didn't act on this, then he might pass up their only chance to make it out of here alive.

Arthur grabbed hold of the door handle and hesitated.

"This will look bright," he said.

"Okay. I understand."

"No," Arthur said. "You don't. I mean *extremely* bright. Blinding."

This time, Niccolo didn't respond. Arthur closed his eyes, steadied his breathing, and threw open the door.

His warning to Niccolo didn't even begin to do justice to the intensity of the light. Even with his eyelids closed as tightly as possible, the illumination felt painful and disorienting. That was the idea, after all. They had been trapped in here for hours, and his adversaries had aimed a huge spotlight directly at the door. His eyes struggled to adjust, and for the moment, he stood completely blind.

Shouts and curses came from further down the hallway, as well as more gunshots. Arthur held up his tranquilizer gun and opened his eyes, but could only see blurry shapes and bright spots ahead of him in the tunnel.

"The door!" the bishop shouted, though Arthur couldn't tell which blur belonged to him.

He picked a blur at random and fired, releasing a dart at what he hoped was the bishop.

He couldn't tell if his dart hit or not, but it looked like something slumped to the ground. His relief came short-lived, however, when something whizzed past his head with a puff of air. An echoing gunshot followed this, and quickly, he stepped back into the room and out of their sightline.

By now, his eyes had adjusted somewhat, and he could see the area around him better. His vision remained blurry, but he didn't have any time to spare.

"Here goes nothing," he said, swinging the door open once more and stepping into the opening.

He trusted his reflexes and hoped he proved faster than his opponent. Arthur picked the other blur and fired, but not before the enemy returned fire as well. A bullet landed. However, since it hit him on the move, the shot only grazed his arm, but it still felt quite painful.

His dart hit, and he let out a hiss of excitement, but nothing happened. He'd hit the man squarely in the chest, but the guy gave no reaction. The guard raised his gun to fire again. Arthur closed his eyes and braced himself against the return shots, fully expecting to die here.

He heard firing but felt nothing.

Maybe his body just became slow to react, but seconds passed, and he still felt no pain or impact. Finally, he opened his eyes once more and stepped into the hallway. Everything had fallen silent.

Off to his right, down the hall, more gunshots sounded. Arthur assumed someone continued to fight over there. He neither knew nor cared what happened or whoever else had become involved. To his left, running footsteps indicated someone headed away.

Once his eyes had adjusted to the bright light fully, he saw that he had dropped a guard. Naomi slumped against the wall, eyes open, and holding her arm.

"Hey, Arthur," she murmured through the pain. On her lap lay a pistol, and the barrel still smoked. "You're welcome."

"Are you all right?"

"It's nice to see you too."

Around her on the floor lay two dead guards. One of them, riddled with bullet holes, leaned against the wall. Another lay on the floor with what looked like a shotgun blast to the chest. The first man had one of Arthur's darts sticking out of his chest.

"Dart gun?" Naomi asked.

"Tranquilizers," Arthur said.

"You brought party drugs to a demon fight?"

He shrugged. "Honestly, I didn't know if they would work or not."

"Then, let's settle that debate. They don't. Next time, bring sparklers and you might have more luck."

"Where did the bishop go?" Niccolo asked.

"Left," Naomi said, pointing down the hallway. "He has his car waiting out there."

"Stay here," Arthur said, sprinting off into the darkness after the bishop.

✳✳✳

Garfield made it up the ladder and back into the treatment plant just as the patrol guard he'd seen earlier came back into the building. The guy looked surprised to see him, which gave Garfield the upper hand. He raised his pistol and fired off two quick shots.

The first hit the man in the shoulder, and the second thudded into his stomach. He collapsed to the ground with a groan but, immediately, picked himself up again.

"More demons?" Garfield said, disgusted. "This hardly seems fair."

The demon fired off return shots and rushed out of sight behind some old pipes to get cover. Garfield cursed at him and lowered his gun. He turned back to the ladder and aimed into the hole. Then he waited for someone to appear in his sightline, grinning.

"Want some of this?" he shouted. "I've got the high ground!"

A second later, something came soaring at him out of the hole. It looked like a little dark orb, and even though he couldn't recognize it in the dim lighting, he felt certain he knew what it was.

He tried to swat at it, a sinking feeling in his stomach, but it remained just out of his reach.

"Uh oh."

He dove behind a huge concrete pillar right before the grenade went off, and the impact hit hard enough to make it feel like a small earthquake had struck in the area beneath him.

Tiny shards of metal tore into the cement wall behind which he hid. Luckily, the huge pillar stood solid, and even though the metal edges chipped away at it, they didn't prove enough to pierce through all the way.

He stood up again, disoriented from the blast, and stumbled away from the access hatch toward the far exit of the building. The guard would be climbing the ladder right now, which meant that Garfield had to get away from it until he could clear the cobwebs from his brain.

To that end, Garfield rushed toward the door leading outside, the one the guard had used earlier. This one stood locked up, unlike the other one, so he fired a few shots into the chain and busted it open.

Garfield stepped out into the cool night air just as the belowground guard made it out of the access hatch and shot at him. The patrol guard he'd hit in the stomach also caught up, and now he had two after him. Both of them, he estimated, were possessed and would prove tough to take down.

He ducked around the side of the building, shaking his head to clear it from the grenade blast. A ringing sound buzzed in his head, and he slammed his palm against his temple to try and clear it.

No dice.

With a curse, he stumbled forward along the building, trying to create some distance from his pursuers, but already, they had rounded the first corner behind him. He aimed over his shoulder and fired.

The shots forced them to duck out of the way. Though he didn't land any hits, Garfield did manage to buy himself a little time.

The gun stopped recoiling, though he couldn't hear the clicking sound of it running empty over the ringing in his ears. He ejected the clip, slid another out of his pocket, and jammed it in with one fluid motion. Then he chambered another round.

Not a moment too soon, either. The two guards had just come around the corner again. Another few shots sent them ducking for cover, and Garfield reached the other end of the building. He ducked around the corner, still trying to clear his head.

***

Arthur rushed down the hallway, which inclined slightly upward as it went. Finally, he came to an outside doorway that he realized exited above ground. It became significantly brighter here, just reaching dusk, and he squinted against the sudden glare of moonlight.

A huge metal door hung open, and it led out into the graveyard of enormous pipes he had seen earlier. Some of them climbed several stories into the air and ran vertically into the buildings surrounding them. Many of them had rusted, and some had holes through them. All of it abandoned and forgotten by the original builders of this facility.

He kept squinting, looking for movement amidst the pipes. The setting sun put most of it in shade, but regardless, he could still see only blurs of motion. To his left, the bishop wove through the maze, dodging around pipes and heading for the other end. Arthur raised his gun, sighted in, and pulled the trigger.

The dart missed the bishop by a few inches, pinging off an exposed pipe like a bell and disappearing into the maze.

Arthur growled in frustration. That had spent the last shot in his gun, but luckily, he had a backup. He tucked his tranquilizer gun away and drew out Niccolo's. Three more chances.

He lost sight of Bishop Glasser in the pipes, but at least now his eyes had adjusted further. Still blurry, but not as bad. He held the tranquilizer gun ready and moved through the area, listening for any sounds from his target.

A flash of movement to the left. Arthur shifted his weight, leaned forward around a pipe, and fired. The dart whistled in and hit the bishop's robes but didn't pierce his skin.

"That was a close one!" the bishop said, and then laughed from up ahead. "You nearly got me."

Arthur ignored the taunt and kept walking, weaving through the pipes and trying to get a clear view of the bishop. Footsteps resounded when the man kept moving forward. Many of the pipes ran together in bunches, some of them big enough around that he could have crawled through them.

"Come now, Arthur. Don't be a sourpuss. We're having

fun."

"I've got Naomi. Your plan is exposed. It's over."

"You think she knows it? She knows nothing. She's of no consequence."

"She knows what you've been up to."

"She knows the *logistics*, but she doesn't know my *purpose*."

"What purpose is that?"

"Tsk tsk. You expect me to give away my entire plan?"

"I had hoped."

Arthur ducked under a pipe, and then quick-stepped to the side, trying to catch a view of the bishop. No such luck, though. Just more pipes.

"How about we play a game where you *guess* what my plan is, and I tell you if you're hot or cold."

"How about you turn yourself in, instead."

"That sounds considerably less fun."

The bishop's voice echoed off the metal and came at him from different sides, making it impossible for Arthur to tell how far away he stood. The pipes confused him, like walking through a field of corn, and he had lost his sense of direction entirely.

Frustrated, Arthur blew out a breath, stepping around another pipe with his gun ready.

"You worked with Naomi," Arthur said. "Niccolo told me about her and what she does for the Church."

"And what is that?"

It would bring a risk mentioning the Vatican Children. If Niccolo had it correct, and the bishop *didn't* know about them, then Arthur could give away important secrets.

Arthur didn't share that theory, however, and he believed that those children were exactly what the bishop had gone after. The only thing he didn't know was *why?*

This offered his best chance to get information from the bishop about his plan for the Vatican Children. He would need to take the risk.

"He told me about the Vatican Children."

"Interesting. You don't disappoint, Arthur. Not in Everett, and not now. How is Desiree? Tell her I haven't forgotten about her. Tell her I *will* come for her." The words oozed with implied meaning. The playful voice had gone, leaving behind only anger.

"You hope to corrupt the children and have them serve your purpose, don't you?"

"Excellent theory. What purpose is that?"

"You want to use them to bring down the Church."

"Oh, I certainly intend to use them *against* the Church," Bishop Glasser said, "but, I don't want to bring it down. Not that. Never that."

"What do you mean?"

"The Church has stood for *Millennia*, Arthur, and it has long provided a beacon of hope in an otherwise dark world. I intend to restore it to the light."

"You've made deals with demons."

"I've enslaved demons," the bishop said. "There is an important distinction. And if you think the Church has never done questionable things to serve the greater good, then perhaps you need a lesson in history."

"What purpose do these children serve?"

"They offer our future," the bishop said. "Long ago, they became our leaders and our weapons. We cultivated them and utilized their gifts to improve the world."

"You made them murderers?"

"Among other things. There remained so few that men cherished each one. Now, though, the population has exploded, and we can reach them all over the world. This gift from God can help us right the wrongs of the world. So, what does the Church do? We track down the children and then ignore them. We let them live unfulfilled lives never even *knowing* the gift that God has given them. I don't intend to squander their gifts anymore. With them, we can rise again."

"Rise? It seems to me that you are a bottom feeder. Nothing more than a petty murderer. You slaughtered my family," Arthur said. "You are a monster."

"Maybe, but I needed allies. Your family was convenient."

"And so what, your influence had run out? Was that why you planned to murder Aram's family in Everett?"

"Oh, no," the bishop said. "That situation was *quite* different."

Arthur stepped around another pipe, but still found no sign of the bishop. He figured that by now they must have neared the far end of the maze, and then nowhere would remain for the bishop to hide.

"Different how?"

"I had no intention of killing both of Aram's children. One, yes. The sister had no value. Haatim, on the other hand ... I would never harm a hair on his head."

A chill ran up Arthur's spine. "What?"

"He's special," the bishop said. "*He* is the one for whom I've searched. Since I began this project, he's the strongest child I've seen."

The sound of a car starting came from up ahead. Arthur cursed and rushed forward, dodging through the pipes as fast as he could.

"Ah, my ride!" the bishop shouted. "I've had fun chatting with you, Arthur, but I must get on my way."

Arthur stepped out of the pipes and onto an access road just as the bishop climbed into the back of a black car. Arthur raised Niccolo's tranquilizer gun and fired—but too late. The dart went into the car at an angle and tore into the passenger seat, and then the door closed all the way.

The car sped off.

Arthur considered firing his last shot. Could he break the windshield with it? No point in wasting the dart, though. The metal tips didn't have much strength, and even if he did break the glass, he wouldn't have any shots left with which to hit the bishop.

The taillights disappeared down the road. Arthur cursed, and then headed back toward the graveyard of pipes. Off in the distance, more gunshots sounded. Whoever had helped bust him out of the underground trap, it seemed like they could use some assistance.

He took off at a sprint around the building, heading toward those gunshots.

****

Garfield ran low on rounds, and his mind remained disoriented and fuzzy. These mercenaries worked efficiently, and with demons along for the ride, it made them more formidable still. The two guards behind him hadn't slowed at all, and he struggled just to stay far enough ahead to make a difficult target for them.

He wouldn't manage to keep running like this for long. Hopefully, the pursuit wouldn't land a lucky shot, but the more chances they had, the more likely one would hit its target.

Winded, Garfield rounded another corner of the building and found an old wooden barrel behind which to duck. He steadied his breathing, held his pistol ready, and waited.

Before long, the guards came charging around the corner. They hadn't expected him to stop, which gave him a chance to ambush them. He sighted down on one of them, aiming for the man's vitals.

Then he pulled the trigger, dropping one of the guards with three shots to the chest and head, but the other one reacted at speed and dove behind the corner and out of his sightline. Garfield fired at him, hoping to land a shot.

And then a click sounded when his gun ran dry. The fact that his hearing had returned brought small consolation against the realization that he had run out of bullets and hadn't brought any more clips with him. His knife became all he had left, which would do little good against the assault rifle his opponent carried.

He had wounded this one in the stomach, which meant it remained possible he would bleed out eventually, but that wouldn't happen anytime soon.

With a groan, Garfield ducked back behind the barrel, dropping the pistol and drawing the knife. He would need to wait for his opponent to get close before attacking, but it would bring an extreme risk.

Eyes closed, he steadied his breathing and listened for approaching footsteps. His blood pumped in his ears, and that faint ringing sound still buzzed from the earlier explosion. Apart from that, he could hear little else.

Knife held ready, he strained to hear and held his breath, but nothing happened. A few seconds passed, and those turned into a minute. Cautiously, he raised himself up over the barrel to look. The mercenary lay on the ground.

Near him and watching Garfield with a bemused expression on his face, stood Arthur Vangeest. He held what looked like a modified pistol.

Garfield stood and slipped his knife away, ignoring the fact that his hand trembled ever so slightly.

"Hey, Garfield. Long time, no see."

"Same, Arthur. Never thought I would say this," he said, "but, boy, am I glad to see you."

Chapter 12

Arthur knelt to pick up the dart from the mercenary who he'd just shot in the neck. It came as a relief that this dart had worked, unlike the last one, and he attributed it to the fact that the man had received wounds already.

The darts cost a lot, and it proved a heck of a lot cheaper to refill one than to keep buying new ones. He lamented all the lost darts he'd fired into the graveyard of pipes, but they didn't have time to go searching in there.

In his pocket, he had two more full darts, so he took a moment to reload them into the chamber of his tranquilizer gun just in case. Garfield watched him, a smirk on his face. It made a tedious and cumbersome process to slide the darts in perfectly. He felt almost sure he wouldn't need them since the bishop had gone already, but he didn't know if any more surprises waited for him.

Part of him—a large part, if he were honest—wanted to grab the rifle from the downed guard and carry that instead. He didn't, though. Arthur had committed to his promise to himself not to kill anymore.

"You brought a dart gun out here?"

"Tranquilizer," Arthur said. "Top-of-the-line model."

"You've got to be kidding me," Garfield muttered, rising to a full standing posture from behind the barrel.

He looked exhausted and disheveled and as if he hadn't showered in weeks, which wouldn't bring anything new where Garfield was concerned. He drank too much and acted anti-social, but he also made a damned good Hunter.

"Saved your ass, didn't it?" Arthur said.

"Does that thing even work on demons?"

"Worked this time, didn't it?"

"This time? So, you don't know?"

"Your guess is as good as mine," Arthur said. "Hit one earlier, and it didn't do squat, but this one seemed to work."

"I wounded him already." Garfield gestured toward the various holes in the guard's chest.

"Your point?"

"Maybe he ran out of steam, and your pea shooter didn't do a thing."

Probably true, but Arthur wouldn't give Garfield the satisfaction of admitting it. "Keep telling yourself that," Arthur said, sliding the gun away and heading back toward the doorway out of which he'd come running. He needed to get back to Niccolo and Naomi and find out where the bishop had headed.

He needed to gather Niccolo up and get out of here. They couldn't afford to let the bishop get too much of a lead on them, not when Arthur knew the plan now.

Garfield fell into step beside him.

"I will keep telling myself that. I would have managed fine on my own."

"Sure."

"What the hell were you doing out here, anyway?"

"Frieda didn't tell you?"

"Does she ever?" Garfield rolled his eyes. "She gave me the gist of it, but no specifics. She just told me to jump."

"I came on a job."

"What job could have you hunting down a bishop? And without the Church's permission, no less."

"It doesn't matter."

"Like hell it doesn't."

"Don't worry about it," Arthur said. "I appreciate the assist, but I'll take things from here."

"So that's how you want to play this?" Garfield asked, an edge of anger in his voice. "Mr. Super Important doesn't want to fill me in about just what in the hell he's doing at a water treatment plant outside California with a priest and chasing down a bishop? I thought we worked on the same side, Arthur?"

Arthur sighed, rubbing his forehead. "I've got things under control."

"Sure as hell seems that way. I gave up a Wendigo to come save your ass. Just tell me what the hell is going on.

What the hell is Naomi doing working with the Catholic Church?"

"I honestly don't know," Arthur said.

"But you have some ideas?"

"Yeah," Arthur said. "Some."

Then he fell silent. They had almost reached where Niccolo waited, watching Naomi. Bullet holes riddled the walls from the earlier fight, and the entire tunnel smelled of blood. One of the men that had gotten shot—by Garfield no doubt—had ended up ripped apart by buckshot, leaving a horrifying mess.

Naomi sat up now and patched up her arm. She looked like she'd lost a fair amount of blood, but she would be fine. Her expression soured when she saw Garfield with Arthur. Niccolo sat on the floor, staring at nothing, and he jumped when Arthur touched him on the shoulder. "Did you get the bishop?"

"No," Arthur said. "He had a car waiting and got out of here."

"Where is he going?"

Arthur looked over at Naomi. "That's what we need to find out."

"Don't give me that look, Arthur," Naomi said. "I saved your ass."

"How do you figure?"

"Glasser wanted to go in and kill you both, and I talked him into just waiting. I tried to get him to let you walk. If we'd rushed in when he wanted us to, you would have been screwed."

"I can take care of myself."

"Not with your pea shooter," Garfield said.

"When I saw it was you down here in the tunnels, I knew Frieda would send backup," she said. Then she looked at Garfield. "I just didn't think it would take so *long*."

"Two states away," Garfield said. "You're lucky I came at all."

"This is all quite amusing, but *where* is the bishop

headed?" Niccolo said. "We need to find him before he slips away for good."

"He's going to his family," Naomi said. "The children he made me help him kidnap."

"Why did you help him?" Niccolo asked. "When the Church finds out—"

"He *was* the Church," Naomi said, cutting him off with a raised hand. She picked herself up from the wall, moving awkwardly with only the one good arm. "I worked with him for years, and he said he'd passed the information on to the Vatican. Until a few months ago that remained true."

"What do you mean?"

"The Church assigned him to work with me. We would find children, and he would bring the names and locations back to the Vatican. He acted as my handler, one of several I've worked with over the years. A few months ago, he started acting strange, but we just kept collecting the names. Then I found out he had nabbed the children after I told him a target instead of taking them to the Church."

"You mean he kidnapped them?"

Garfield cut in, "Kidnapping *who?* Children?"

"Yes," Naomi said. "Children."

Garfield looked over at Arthur. "That's what you meant? The idea you had about what was going on."

"It's worse than you think," Arthur said, nodding at Naomi. "Keep talking."

She nodded. "About a month ago, I asked the Vatican about the missing children to see if something had changed, and they acted like they had no idea what was going on. They accused *me* of shirking my duties and said no names had been delivered in months. Glasser had reported me MIA to the Church even while he kidnapped the kids."

"So, they didn't believe you?" Arthur asked.

"When I told them about the kidnapped children, it became my word against Glasser's. They asked him some questions, he denied the allegations, and that brought the end of it. Needless to say, that didn't end well for me, and they gave me an ultimatum to shape up or face the consequences."

"So you helped him grab the kids," Arthur said.

"At that point, I still didn't know what he had planned for them. It seemed messed up, but I've done worse things in the past and didn't want the Church pissed at me."

"How many?" Niccolo asked. "How many children did you help him kidnap?"

Naomi hesitated. "A dozen," she said. "At least. I found out that he grabbed a few of them long before I thought things had started. They've been with him for years."

"Where are they?"

"All around," she said. "He's planted them in different cities throughout the states to get as wide a coverage as possible."

"Coverage?" Garfield asked. "Coverage for what?"

Niccolo supplied the answer, "Their exposure."

****

"He wants to use the kids to make the world aware that such children exist. Just letting people *know* that things like this are real gives enough to cause widespread panic. He's prepped them for this moment and plans to unleash them on the world," Naomi said.

"You mean killing people."

"Wreaking general havoc." She nodded. "When I found out, I dug deeper and followed him, which is how I know where he will have gone."

"Where?" Arthur asked.

"I need assurances."

"I need information."

"I have it," Naomi said. "So, what will you offer in return?"

Already, Arthur had made his deal with Elgin not to pursue Naomi. He would let her go once this had finished, but she didn't need to know that. The worse she thought her position was, the easier it would prove to get the information he needed.

The problem was that Garfield hadn't made such a similar bargain. He also didn't like to make deals with people, much less people like Naomi. If Arthur tried to cut her a deal in front of him, it could become a problem.

"I'll put in a good word for you with the Council and the Church."

"Not good enough. Your word against my crimes won't balance out too well."

"That's the deal. Take it or leave it."

"Then, I leave it," she said.

"Naomi ..."

"I'm serious, Arthur. Good luck finding the bishop without my help."

Father Niccolo Paladina's voice cut through the air, "Good luck making it out of this tunnel alive if you don't."

***

He spoke quietly, his words barely audible, and they caught Arthur off-guard. The words sounded calm and spoken evenly, but an undercurrent of rage and fear came with them.

They seemed to have a similar effect on Naomi, though she soon recovered from her momentary shock.

"You are a priest. You would never murder me in cold blood."

"No," he said. "You're right. I wouldn't. I don't represent just myself, though. I *represent* the Church. These men work for the Church, and if I tell them to kill you, they will."

Arthur thought to interject and remind Niccolo that he wouldn't kill *anyone* anymore, but he changed his mind. After all, Niccolo only bluffed.

At least, he hoped he did.

Garfield, however, said, "Wrong, Priest. I serve the

Council, and I don't take orders from you."

He waited a beat, drew his pistol, and then continued, "But, in this case, I might make an exception. I have no qualms about killing Naomi myself if she doesn't tell us what we need to know. So, what will it be? Want to try your luck with the Church or with us?"

Naomi gulped, weighing her options. "An hour head start. That's all I ask."

"Hell—" Garfield said.

"Fine," Arthur said. "You give us the information to track down the bishop, and we'll give you a head-start."

"No way." Garfield stepped forward and grabbed Arthur's shoulder. "She tried to *murder* you. Hell, she tried to murder *me*."

"Not me or my men," she said. "Not anymore. The bishop got to them."

Garfield ignored her, lowering his voice so that only Arthur could hear. "I'll not let her go that easily. You get your information, and I take her in."

"The longer this takes, the more of a lead the bishop has," Arthur said quietly. "We can't afford the time."

"We can't afford to give her a head-start like that. She'll slip away."

Arthur argued, "The stakes are way bigger than just her. If we don't stop the bishop, he'll wreak major havoc on the world and hurt the Church and the Council."

"Not my problem," Garfield said. "My job wasn't to come and take orders from you but to help you. You're making the wrong call, and I shan't let you do it."

"The children—"

"I don't care one lick about those kids," Garfield said with a hiss. "We've got Naomi here, which gives us a win. I only care about bringing her in."

"We need the information," Arthur said. "Bishop Glasser has far more importance."

"I'll be damned before I let you send her on her way without any punishment. She helped us out, and I'll make sure the Council knows about that, but I *will not* let her go."

Arthur had feared that, and he didn't want a confrontation with Garfield. However, he'd given Elgin his word that Naomi could walk, and he didn't want to go back on it now.

So, how could he satisfy his commitment to Elgin and keep Garfield happy at the same time?

"Look, Garfield, I know that you answer to the Council and not to me, but I—"

"We'll give you your head-start."

They turned to face Niccolo. The priest held a gun. Not a tranquilizer, though. He had picked up a pistol from one of the downed guards, and now aimed it at Garfield.

The statement, however, he'd directed at Naomi.

"What?" she asked, surprised. "Yeah, definitely. I'm in."

"Ten minutes. You tell us what we need to know, and you get a ten-minute head-start."

"Deal."

Garfield said, "No deal. I sure as hell will not—"

Niccolo narrowed his eyes at him. "Shut up."

Garfield did, but he spent the next few seconds sizing up Niccolo. "You won't shoot me," Garfield said, his tone softer and more sinister. "You barely even know how to hold that thing. Did Arthur teach you *nothing* before tossing you into the deep end?"

"He taught me enough."

"No," Garfield said. "Not *nearly* enough."

"I *will* shoot you. Don't make me do it."

"No, you won't. You're a priest. That would be murder."

"You don't know me."

Arthur stared at Niccolo. The look in the priest's eyes held as much resolve as fear, and it became clear that he had gone in way over his head. A spontaneous decision to seize the moment had become a moment of which he had quickly lost control.

Arthur had to admit that this turn of events surprised him. He wouldn't have expected anything like this from

Niccolo.

"Your hand is shaking," Garfield said. "Just put down the gun, and I'll forget this ever happened."

"No," Niccolo said. He turned back to Naomi. "Tell us, and then go."

She hesitated, and then made her choice, "An hour."

Garfield turned to Arthur. "I just saved your lives. And you allow him to treat me like this?"

"He does what he wants," Arthur said. "You think I can control him?"

"Do we have a deal?" Naomi asked. "An hour."

"Deal," Niccolo said. "Now, tell us what you know."

"You little—"

Garfield turned back to Niccolo and rushed him. From his movement, it grew clear that he meant to body-tackle the priest and wrestle away the gun.

Arthur had expected this and felt glad he'd taken the time to reload his tranquilizer gun. The darts didn't work on demons but remained quite potent against humans.

Arthur fired his last remaining darts into the burly man's back. One shot would have given enough, but two couldn't hurt. Garfield staggered forward an extra couple of steps before collapsing to the ground. He hit his face hard against the cement flooring. It would hurt when he awoke.

"Let's make it two hours," Arthur said, sliding the tranquilizer gun away. Then, he shrugged. "Give or take."

Naomi stared at them in shock, and then burst out laughing. "You really are cold-blooded, aren't you?"

"I've been called worse. Start talking."

"He has a boat to take him out of the country," Naomi said. "But that isn't his only stop. He plans to get the kids and head overseas. A shipping freighter will get him to Europe."

"Why?"

"I don't know," Naomi said. "He's still after one of the kids. An important one that he wants to grab before he starts his little crusade. He said he would handle this one himself."

"Who is the child?" Niccolo asked.

"Some kid named—"

"It doesn't matter," Arthur said. He didn't want Niccolo to know that Haatim Arison had become one of the Vatican Children. "You didn't report any of these children's names to the Vatican, right?"

"No," Naomi said. "But I have the list."

"Give it to me, and I'll make sure it ends up in the right hands."

She nodded, slipping a little notebook out of her pocket and handing it to him. "Good riddance. I don't want to talk to the Church for a while anyway."

In the book, she wrote the address of the house where Bishop Glasser kept the kidnapped children, and then which dock from which he planned to leave.

To use the freighter made sense, because by now, the Church would monitor airline traffic in case he tried to leave the states, but they would have a much harder time of tracking him or his group of children on a ship.

"You said he won't know we're coming?"

"He thinks I've remained obedient these last few months and has no idea I know where he's held the newest kids. And, for definite, he doesn't know I found out about his overseas transport."

"Fine."

"Can I go?" she asked.

"What about the other kids?" Niccolo wanted to know. "The ones he's had for a while."

"The ones he's indoctrinated already have scattered. Their goal, as far as I can tell, is to make headlines and show people what they can do."

"Do you know where they went?"

"No," Naomi said. "A few. Most, you won't have to worry about. Two in particular, though ..."

"What?"

"Let's just say that one of them, in particular, gives me the creeps. He stayed at the bishop's side most of the time and kept an eye on the new kids. They call him Jeremy."

Arthur prompted, "The other one?"

"Ohio," she said. "Whatever he has planned for this kid, it will go down there. She's a telekinetic, I think. Wish I could give you more specifics, but that's all I've got. Now, can I go? My head-start is shortening by the minute."

"If this information doesn't pan out, then I will come find you," Arthur said. "And I'll not feel too happy when I do."

"I wouldn't expect any less, Arthur. The intel' is good, and as long as you hurry, you'll catch him at the docks. If you dally, though, then no promises, so you two want to get moving."

Niccolo exchanged a glance with Arthur.

"So ..." Naomi said. "One last time. Can I *go*?"

"Yeah," Arthur said, waving his hand in dismissal. "Get out of here."

She didn't wait for him to change his mind, just took off running down the hallway toward the maze of pipes, disappearing into the darkness. Though she held her arm where she'd gotten shot, she looked mostly unhurt. Arthur watched her go, and then turned back to Niccolo.

"What about him?" Niccolo asked, gesturing toward Garfield.

Arthur sighed. "Even odds he comes after us when he wakes up. He isn't the forgiving type."

"Should we just leave him?"

Arthur shook his head. "I'll drop him at his car. Least we can do, considering."

He knelt and slung Garfield over his shoulder in a fireman's carry position. It became rough getting him to the exit because he was a big guy, but Arthur felt grateful he wouldn't have to carry him up the ladder.

Niccolo fished around in Garfield's pocket while they walked, and then rushed ahead to get his car. Arthur figured it would sit parked close to his, and he was right. Niccolo came back a couple of minutes later.

"He buried it under some branches," he said. "Took me a minute to find it."

Arthur put Garfield on the backseat. The guy would have a bruised jaw and even more bruised ego, but otherwise, would be okay. On a whim, Arthur popped open his trunk to see what lay inside.

A whole arsenal. Rifles, shotguns, pistols, explosives, and more. Greater firepower than he could imagine using in a few years on the job.

Arthur wanted to take some with him. If this situation had taught him anything, it was that no matter how much he hated the murderer he used to be, he hated being helpless even more. For sure, walking into this situation unprepared had nearly gotten him killed—something he didn't want to do again.

On the other hand, taking the guns out of Garfield's trunk would take a resounding step backward. It would signify that his change hadn't worked and would effectively mean giving up. He didn't want to give up and go back to the murderer he had been.

In the end, he compromised and took holy water, salt, and other implements he could use against demons, but left the weapons alone. He did take a shotgun loaded with rock-salt shells, but that made the extent of the firepower.

When he closed the trunk, he saw that Niccolo stood staring at him. The priest didn't say anything, but the look of approval on his face made his feelings on the matter known. He nodded at Arthur, who nodded back, and then they walked out to their car still parked out of the way.

On the walk, Arthur called Frieda, but it went straight to voicemail. He left a quick message, asking her to tell Garfield he felt sorry for leaving him but that he didn't have any other options, and then he hung up.

A few minutes later and they got on the road.

✳✳✳

In silence, they drove toward the address Naomi had given them. Niccolo, exhausted from the recent hours trapped underground as well as his recent burst of adrenaline, kept replaying the events in his mind from when he'd aimed the gun at Garfield. He hardly believed that he had done that—it felt like a dream, as if he watched someone else.

He wouldn't have shot him, of course, but had just bluffed to win over Naomi. Niccolo had kept the gun, tucking it into his belt, but couldn't settle on why. It didn't come down to a conscious decision he'd made, and he chalked it up to exhaustion. He could barely keep his head up and now ran on fumes. Oh, to take a break and have a soft bed into which to fall.

More discouraging still, Arthur—seated in the driver's seat beside him—didn't look much better. And spending so many hours trapped in those underground tunnels had cost them in more than time. They couldn't afford to slow down or stop. They knew where the bishop had headed and couldn't afford to miss him.

"I didn't expect that from you," Arthur said, breaking the silence.

Niccolo hadn't expected it either—pulling the gun on Garfield had happened on a spur-of-the-moment decision. One he had regretted instantly. It had almost backfired, and if Arthur hadn't reacted the way he did to intervene, then Niccolo would have only managed to make the situation much worse.

"We didn't have a lot of time, and we couldn't afford to argue with him anymore about it," Niccolo said.

"Not with innocent children on the line," Arthur said. "I didn't say you made the wrong choice, just an unexpected one."

"I'm not sure you understand what's at stake," Niccolo said. "It isn't just about the children but about humanity as a whole."

"What do you mean?"

"People like to read about witches, warlocks, and demons in stories, but things like that aren't *supposed* to exist. Not out in the real world. Think of the inquisition, or what happened in Salem, and what happens to good people when they think the supernatural has reality. If these children go through with the bishop's plan ... they'll set off a chain-reaction of fear like people have experienced throughout history. They'll get torn apart, and that will only make a beginning."

"Not if we get to them first," Arthur said. "I can send the information to Frieda, and she'll get Hunters tracking these kids immediately. As soon as we figure out exactly what the bishop's plan is, we can stop it."

"We might end up too late."

"We won't."

"But, we might." Niccolo shook his head. "I keep thinking back to what Desiree said, and now what Naomi said. Both of them came to the Church for help, and both of them got turned away."

"Mistakes were made."

"It's more than that," Niccolo said. "The Church shouldn't turn *anyone* away when they come seeking help. We allowed this to happen, all of it. Signs appeared years ago that Bishop Glasser couldn't be trusted, and yet they elevated him."

"The world isn't fair," Arthur said. "And people let you down. People make mistakes, and they *will* let you down. All you can do is pick yourself back up, dust yourself off, and keep moving forward."

"Spoken by a man who tried to get himself killed in West Virginia when he raided that occult den."

Arthur's eyes went wide. "How did you ...?"

"It wasn't a difficult thing to surmise. You went in there with no intention of coming out, didn't you? What do you know about *moving* forward?"

Arthur didn't respond straight away, and Niccolo could tell his words had wounded the other man.

"I'm sorry," he said. "That was uncalled for."

"It's all right. You aren't wrong, but I'm not that man anymore. People change, and sometimes for the better."

Niccolo changed the subject, "I can't believe the Church would allow something like this."

"I can. Men make up the Church. God might be divine, but men make mistakes. Men are corruptible."

Niccolo didn't have a good response to that. He'd put his faith, his life, and his future in the hands of the Church. He'd given up everything to serve as a priest and an exorcist for the Vatican, and for the first time in his life, he wondered if he might have made a mistake.

***

Whatever Arthur had expected to find when they reached the house Naomi had sent them to, the rundown little building they parked in front of wasn't it at all. It looked as if tenants had abandoned it years ago and, perhaps, forfeited it to squatter's rights. The broken-down affair had shattered windows and rotting wood and looked like a strong breeze might knock it over.

"*This* is where he's keeping the children?" Niccolo muttered a little prayer under his breath, though Arthur couldn't make out the words.

"Looks like," Arthur said.

He opened the door and climbed out into the hot California morning. They had driven for the last several hours, and the sun had only just begun to rise. Arthur had managed to sleep a little in the tunnels before Garfield rescued them, but aside from that, he had remained awake for almost thirty-six hours straight.

His body felt sore, and his muscles cramped, but he had to admit, after so many hours stuck in that underground hole, he felt quite a bit better now. He would take miserable and exhausted out in the morning air over getting trapped and desperate like a rat in a maze any day.

"Do you think he has guards?"

"Most likely," Arthur said, picking up the tranquilizer gun. "Or, at least, there were guards. It doesn't look like anyone is here now."

"You think he's gathered the children already and gone on his way to the docks?"

"Only one way to find out."

Arthur loaded in three new darts, and then walked toward the door. Niccolo's tranquilizer gun lay in the backseat, having run out of compressed air, so he didn't bother reloading it. He only had one more backup canister, and he figured it best to save it for now.

"Stay behind me," Arthur said.

With the gun behind his back, out of sight, he climbed the creaking steps and knocked on the front door of the hovel and waited.

Nothing happened. No sounds or motion from inside the house. He knocked again, waited, and then let out a sigh.

"Gone," he said.

"We should keep moving."

"Let's check first," Arthur said. "See if we can find any clues about where he put the other children around the country."

"We don't have a lot of time."

"I know," Arthur said. "But, the boat shouldn't leave for four hours, and it will only take us two to reach the docks."

He reached forward, tested the doorknob, and found it unlocked. Gently, he pushed it open, tranquilizer gun held ready, but the interior proved empty and silent.

"Anyone here?" Niccolo asked.

"No," Arthur said. "Stay here and keep an eye outside. I'll do a quick sweep, and then we can go."

He didn't wait for Niccolo to answer before moving deeper into the rundown home and searching for any clues as to the bishop's plans. From what Naomi had said, the most dangerous child had gone to Ohio, but several more also made a part of the bishop's plan. All of them needed stopping.

A lot of abandoned items made it clear that all of the occupants had left in a hurry. Macaroni and cheese packets or hotdogs made up most of the foodstuffs he found in the trash, and from some of the toys and paraphernalia that he discovered scattered, he realized that some of the children were rather young indeed.

That would slow the bishop, having to watch after them and keep young children from straying. With luck, that would mean he and Niccolo didn't stay too far behind.

It would take another short drive to get to the dock that Naomi had mentioned. Arthur had hoped to gain some clue about what to expect from the children that the bishop had kidnapped, but so far, nothing had sprung to mind. It made it difficult to know how to prepare when he had no idea of the children's capabilities, or whether or not they would stay loyal to the bishop.

He gave the home an extra cursory sweep to see if any papers or information remained that they might use to help locate the other children, but he didn't see anything promising. Unlike the last time he'd invaded the bishop's manner, on this occasion, he took care in cleaning up when he left.

Arthur made it back out front where Niccolo waited.

"Nothing," he said, sliding the gun away and heading for the car.

"What now?"

"We need to get to the dock," Arthur said. "Once we have the bishop, we can find out what he planned and where the other children went."

Niccolo didn't object but rather climbed into the passenger seat of the car. Arthur had them back on the freeway in only a few minutes, heading out toward the docks to the northwest.

"And then what?" Niccolo asked.

"What do you mean?"

"What do we do with the bishop?" the priest said.

"We turn him over to the Church," Arthur said. "And then we go and stop the children before anything bad happens."

"We turn him over so they can just let him loose again?"

Arthur didn't answer. He could sympathize with the sort of crisis of faith that Niccolo experienced. It brought pain for him to realize that the institution that had raised him had also let him down.

Arthur didn't have time for it, however. They had a clear job to do, and he needed to make sure Niccolo wouldn't become a distraction in the coming conflicts.

"We'll cross that bridge when we come to it," Arthur said. "For now, stay focused."

Niccolo stared out through the window and didn't reply.

Chapter 13

By the time they made it to the docks, it had grown cloudy and overcast. With a storm on the way, the wind had picked up and whipped around them. It hadn't started raining yet, but it would only take a matter of time before it came down in force.

Niccolo stayed much quieter than usual during the drive, and Arthur worried about him. These last few days, beginning with everything that had happened in Everett and culminating in the tunnels at the water treatment plant, had taken its toll on him. In particular, it had knocked his faith. He had, summarily, learned about the existence of evil forces that wanted him dead, and then found out that they paled in comparison to the evils humanity could wreak upon themselves.

Arthur still had to deal with his own crisis of conscience; though, he had to admit, he felt a small bit of ironic satisfaction in knowing that Niccolo, the perfect little priest that had spent so many months judging him as a monster, had become the one questioning his faith.

"What now?"

"The ship won't leave for a few hours," Arthur said. "We need to find the bishop and the children before they get loaded."

"Maybe the time has arrived to bring the Church in on this."

"What?"

"Should I call the Vatican?" Niccolo asked. "And warn them about events?"

"If you do that," Arthur said, "they will order us to stand down and let them deal with it."

"I won't stand down."

"Then, do you want to disobey a direct order from them? If you make the call, you'll have to do that."

Niccolo didn't reply, but the look on his face gave answer enough. Conflicted, the idea of disobedience wasn't as hard for him to wrap his head around as usual. It led to a slippery slope, Arthur knew, and if Niccolo didn't take care, then very soon, it wouldn't only be small offenses on the table.

That seemed neither here nor there. Right now, they had a clear agenda to accomplish, and they could worry about existential questions of right and wrong later.

With a frown, Arthur looked down at the tranquilizer gun in his hand.

"These have only minimal effect on demons," he said.

"But they have some effect?"

He shrugged. "Some. Maybe."

"You think the bishop might be possessed?"

"I don't think so."

"Me neither. I think he's doing all of this because he wants to. He thinks he's on some mission from God to wake the world. He will use the demons to accomplish his goal, but he would *never* let one of them inside of *him*."

"I agree," Arthur said. "So, the darts should work."

He wished he had another weapon, but for now, the tranquilizer darts would need to work. After all this ended, he could rethink his load-out so he could become more prepared for dealing with demons, but today, this would have to do.

He climbed out of the car and headed toward the shipyard where the bishop and his children would wait to board. The only docked freighter looked massive, nearly the size of a cruise ship, and the hull stood at least eight stories above the water.

Niccolo followed him as they approached. Arthur kept them out of sight of the few workers in the yard as they made their way forward.

"Do you think Glasser is on board?"

"Possibly," Arthur said. "He could have hidden out somewhere nearby, though, still waiting to get on."

"Why is the shipyard so empty?"

"Off-season," Arthur said. "They won't ship much

through here until next year. Skeleton crew until then.”

“We should split up and search for the bishop.”

“No,” Arthur said. “Stick with me.”

“We’ll cover more ground if we separate.”

“The bishop probably has friends, and we don’t know the extent of these kids’ capabilities just yet. They remain dangerous, so you’ll need to stick with me until we can make sure everything is safe.”

Clearly, Niccolo didn’t like the plan, but he didn’t object.

“Where to, then?”

“Follow me.”

Arthur wanted to check the manifest on the ship to see where it was headed—in case they missed the bishop—so he went to what he hoped was a nearby office. He also hoped that he might find some information about who—or what—they transported to get some clue as to where the bishop might have gone.

The accommodations consisted of two prefab one-story structures on top of trailers that looked rickety and had been modified to stick together. With the wheels removed, they sat on top of cinder blocks. A rotting wooden ramp led up to the doorway of the rightmost trailer. The lights remained off, and it appeared empty.

Arthur made sure no one lurked in the area and then made his way up the ramp. The door stood locked, but it only took him a few seconds to pick it and let himself in. Niccolo closed the door behind them.

“What should we look for?”

“I’ll tell you when I find it.”

Arthur made his way over to a stack of papers and documents. He sifted through the stack until he found the manifest he wanted. It belonged to the cargo freighter and had no listed passengers—just what he had expected. The bishop had made some deal to get him and his children on board and hoped to stay undetected during this trip.

They would hide out, though, during the overseas trip,

and he would need a safe place to keep the children. Arthur scanned the paperwork until he found the area of the ship they would likely choose.

"Crew quarters," Arthur said, sliding the manifest into his pocket. "If they've boarded already, then we will find them there."

"Actually," Niccolo said, looking out of the window. "I don't think they got on board yet."

"Why do you say that?"

Arthur walked over to the window beside the priest. In the distance, he could see a lot with about a dozen cars parked in it, though enough spaces remained for several hundred cars at least.

"Third car from the left." Niccolo pointed. "I think I saw some movement."

Arthur counted the cars over. The vehicle that Niccolo indicated seemed similar to the one he had seen speeding away from the water treatment facility earlier that night.

"Stay here," Arthur said. "I'll go and check it out."

He grabbed a yellow work vest from a wall hook and headed back outside the office. Drizzle fell, but lightly. Arthur made his way toward the parking lot and the bishop's car.

He took care to keep the walls of shipping containers between himself and the vehicle so that whoever sat inside wouldn't see him coming. He passed a lone worker checking a couple of containers, but the man merely nodded at him in his worker's vest. Arthur nodded back and kept moving.

Cautious, he circled behind the line of vehicles, ducked low, and made his way up to the front. When he got closer, he saw that Niccolo had guessed correctly. Someone occupied the driver's seat of the car.

The bishop.

Unfortunately, *only* the bishop sat in the vehicle, and no signs showed that any of the children had come with him. The driver who had chauffeured him away earlier didn't seem present either. The car engine was off, and the bishop had cracked open the windows. It looked as if he sat waiting and watching for something.

Arthur drew his gun, crept up to the car, and aimed his weapon through the small aperture.

"Open the door, slowly."

The bishop looked up at him; first, with a look of surprise, and then annoyance.

"That clever bitch."

"Open it," Arthur said.

Instead, the bishop reached forward for the keys, trying to turn on the car. Arthur fired, hitting him in the shoulder with one of his darts. The bishop slumped forward, his body going limp almost immediately.

Not a demon, then. That meant a good thing.

Arthur tested the handle of the car and, happily, found it unlocked. Gently, he opened the door, careful to catch the bishop when he spilled out. He opened the back door, slid the bishop inside, and then got into the driver's seat.

Then he inched the car through the docks toward the office. A few of the milling workers gave him funny looks, but they saw he wore a vest and just shrugged it off. They didn't seem to care overly much about what went on and, probably, would soon clock out for the night before the storm hit.

Arthur parked in front of the makeshift office, waited until no one paid attention, and then carried the bishop inside. When he opened the door, Niccolo gave him a shocked look, but then he helped him move the bishop to a chair.

"You got him?"

"He didn't put up much of a fight."

"What about the children?"

Arthur shook his head. "No sign of them."

"We need to find them."

"I know," Arthur said, nodding toward the bishop. "Now, we can."

"Then we need to wake him."

"It'll take at least an hour to get the stuff out of his system, and then he'll stay groggy a bit longer."

"An hour?" Niccolo asked. "Isn't there, like, an antidote or something?"

Arthur laughed. "No. It isn't poison, just horse tranquilizer. His body needs to metabolize it."

"What do we do until then?"

Arthur shrugged. "We wait."

✱✱✱

While they waited, the drizzle morphed to heavy sheets of rain. The thin walls and ceiling of this office meant that the sound of the downpour drowned out any attempts at easy conversation.

Arthur discovered some tape and tied the bishop to the chair, placing him in the center of the room. Niccolo paced back and forth in silence, arms folded behind his back and an intense expression on his face.

The deluge turned into a full-on thunderstorm, and cracks of thunder rolled overhead as the wind picked up. The lights flickered, and the makeshift hut felt like it might turn into kindling around them, but miraculously, it held up under the storm.

The rough weather passed as quickly as it came on; though, outside, it remained dark and dreary. Most of the crew working on the docks disappeared, and the entire place grew quiet around them.

"Hello again," the bishop said suddenly, his voice splitting the silence. Only about thirty-five minutes had elapsed since Arthur had drugged him, and it surprised the Hunter to see him awake already.

Awake and alert, in fact. The drugs should have taken much longer to get out of his system.

Niccolo exchanged a glance with Arthur, but he could only shrug in response.

"Where are the children?" Niccolo asked.

"Safe."

"Where?"

"I don't know."

"Yes, you do."

The bishop smiled. "No, actually. I don't. I know they are on their way and will get here soon, but they come of their own accord with my driver. I believe they stopped to get ice cream. They come willingly."

"No, they don't," Niccolo said. "They remain your prisoners."

"Is that what you think?" Leopold asked. "Is that what you *truly* believe? You think I took these children against their will and forced their powers upon them?"

"I know you kidnapped them."

"It is true that, at first, they made unwilling participants, but all of that changed when I offered them the key to unlocking their abilities. Once I showed them the truth about who they were, I gave them the choice to stay or go. Every single one of them stayed with me of their own accord."

"I don't believe you."

"And, you do not have to. You have your truth, and I have mine. However, you will see for yourself soon enough."

"Why travel to Europe?"

"It makes just one leg on my journey to India."

"Why? What's in India?"

Bishop Glasser stared at Niccolo for a second, and then turned his attention to Arthur. "You didn't tell him?"

"Tell me what?" Niccolo glanced between the two.

The bishop had backed Arthur into a corner. He'd hoped to keep the information about Aram's son private—he didn't like the Councilman, but he also didn't want the Church to know about his son if they didn't need to—but it had now become too late for that.

"Haatim Arison," Arthur said. "His father is a member of the Council of Chaldea, and he's one of the Vatican Children."

"What? How do you know?"

"The bishop attempted to capture him in Everett before he fled. Those demons all formed part of his plan to capture Haatim."

"Which you both screwed up for me," the bishop said. "But, it is of no consequence because I *will* have him."

Niccolo continued staring at Arthur, a look of confusion and betrayal on his face. "You knew?"

"I didn't want the Church to find out about Haatim. I wanted to keep him off their lists."

"Why?"

"What good has ever come from ending up on a list like that? It doesn't matter," Arthur said. "All I know is that he is one of the Vatican Children."

Bishop Glasser laughed. "Not just one of them. He is *the* one. The only one that matters."

"What?" Niccolo stared.

"I've searched and searched for one like him for *years*. They only come along once every couple of generations, but suffice to say, he will become my crowning achievement. The most important child I've ever met, and he sat right under the Church's nose *this entire time*."

"Does his father know?" Niccolo asked.

"No. Aram has no idea," Arthur said. "He doesn't have any awareness that his child has special abilities."

"And now, Arthur, I know what you must be wondering. You stand there thinking what about your daughter? Was she special, too? Is that *why* she died?"

Arthur hesitated, burning to know the answer to that question. The bishop had it right, though; he felt too afraid to ask. Felt too afraid to know the answer.

And, still, he said, "Was it?"

Bishop Glasser burst out laughing. "Heavens, no. Your daughter was just an insignificant whelp. A convenience."

"Before a few weeks ago, I had never even *heard* of you. What could I possibly have done to you to make you want to kill my wife and daughter?"

"Nothing."

"Nothing? Then why would you murder my family?"

"I didn't. The Ninth Circle did."

"But you gave away their location. You told The Ninth Circle of my family and where to find them."

The bishop shrugged, the movement diminished by the tape. "I needed allies, and they helped me. They taught me how to summon the demons and bind them, though I soon surpassed them when I found Jeremy. Your family proved a small price to pay, in the grand scheme of things. I got the better end of that deal."

"Small price?" Arthur's hands shook in rage.

"I'm sure *you* don't feel that way, but you must look at the larger picture. You had enemies, and they wanted to harm you. I'm sure they regret their choice now, considering what you did to *them* in response, but at that moment, I'm certain they felt quite proud of what they achieved."

"So, killing my family just made for a convenience for you?"

"Did you think it would be anything different? Did you think them special or part of some bigger agenda? The cult would have taken any name from that list of Hunter's families, but yours ended up the only one Emily was stupid enough to give me. I suppose I did you a favor, though. I broke your ties and freed you from that wife and daughter. I freed you to become all you can become, and look what you have achieved!"

Arthur couldn't contain his anger. He stepped forward and punched the bishop on the mouth. Before he could stop himself, he had hit him two more times. Finally, Niccolo caught his arm and pulled him back, a worried look on his face.

The bishop's head lolled to the side, and blood ran down his lip. His eyes refocused, and he looked at Arthur.

"There you go!" Leopold said, laughing. He turned his head and spat a glob of blood onto the office floor. "How does that feel? Does hitting me make you feel any better?"

Arthur cursed and turned, rushing out of the room and into the adjacent trailer before he lost his temper again. Never in his entire life had he felt so furious and out of control.

Niccolo stared at him as he left, but he didn't much care what the priest thought at that moment.

The way the bishop explained the murder of his family ... it cut him to the core. It gave the answer he had feared, but hearing the man speak so casually about their deaths brought all the pain back to him in an unbearable rush.

Arthur staggered around the corner of the trailer and fell against the wall. Slowly, he allowed himself to slide to a sitting position on the floor. His breathing came in short gasps while he fought to regain control of his emotions, but he lost the battle.

A few moments passed, and then Niccolo appeared in the doorway in front of him. He wore a concerned and hesitant expression. "Are you okay?"

"I'm fine." Arthur pushed his hands through his hair and coughed. "I'll come back in there in a minute. Keep an eye on him and don't let him out of your sight."

Niccolo moved to turn, and then hesitated. "Do you think it's true?" Niccolo asked. "What he said about the Vatican Children? Do you think they joined with him willingly?"

"I think some did," Arthur said. "I also think some only want a way out of this nightmare. As hard as he might try, he couldn't make all of them evil."

"We need to find out where they went," Niccolo said. "And then get them to the Church."

"If the bishop told it true," he said, "and some of the kids have become willing servants, then we won't need to look for them at all. Not while we have the bishop."

"What do you mean? Why won't we need to look for them?"

Arthur looked up at him and sighed. "Because they'll find us."

Chapter 14

"What do we do now?" Niccolo asked when Arthur, finally, walked back into the main office where they held the bishop. He had grown anxious and a bit worried. The bishop had something about him that Niccolo hadn't noticed the first time they'd met, and it grated on his nerves. Just occupying the same room with the man filled him with dread.

It remained windy outside and sprinkled, but the storm had almost died down. It didn't feel like the storm had finished, though, but rather that they had entered a lull. They had entered the eye of the storm.

Arthur didn't answer him immediately, which came as no surprise for Niccolo. There didn't seem any good answer for the situation. While catching the bishop had seemed relatively easy, it had brought them no closer to locating the children.

On top of that, he hadn't given them any further information about his plans for the children he had so carefully cultivated. The name he'd heard Naomi say earlier, Jeremy, sounded familiar ... but Niccolo couldn't quite place it. He'd heard it before but couldn't pinpoint where.

They also didn't have any clear answers about what the bishop wanted to accomplish. His endgame couldn't just come down to letting the world know about the existence of Vatican Children. He had to have some ulterior motive, or maybe, a power grab in mind once the world imploded.

"I don't know," Arthur said, at last. "We need to find the children, and then turn them all over to the Church."

"He knows their location but won't tell."

"Have patience."

"I can't have patience," Niccolo said, feeling a burst of frustration. "Don't you *understand* what is at stake? The very foundation of the Church is at risk. Once people know about these children, they will ask questions, and the deeper they dig, the worse things will get for all of us. This situation is terrible in *every* way."

"He won't just offer up the information we need," Arthur said.

"Not willingly," Niccolo said, speaking quietly.

Arthur hesitated, his expression darkening. "What, *exactly,* are you asking?"

"We *need* that information, Arthur. The longer this takes, the more likely that those children will slip through our fingers."

"Say the words, then. Tell me what you want."

"You know what I mean."

"What, then? You want to beat it out of him? You expect me to torture him until he tells us what we want to know?"

"If we must."

"You mean if *I* must," Arthur said, angry. "You wouldn't deign to get your hands dirty, would you?"

"I wouldn't even know where to begin."

"You don't just begin with something like that. And there I thought we had lines we wouldn't cross."

"Normally, we wouldn't, and I *hate* to ask this of you, to *become* something like that. This brings extenuating circumstances."

Niccolo felt surprised that Arthur argued with him about this. He had expected something like relief from the man, not an objection, to the idea of torturing the bishop.

"Does it?" Arthur asked. "If this is the situation we find ourselves in, then what *aren't* extenuating circumstances? If the line in the sand is movable, then what about the time something bad happens, and we need to do terrible things? I seem to recall that the road to hell isn't paved with extenuating circumstances."

"We *need* to get those kids back, Arthur. It's the only thing that matters right now."

"Is it?"

"Yes!"

"You think torture is the way to do it? How, exactly, did you imagine it going? You would step outside, and I would take care of everything? Did you imagine I would cut his arms and legs to get him to talk? Or maybe smash his fingers and toes one at a time until he gives us the information we need?"

"I don't know."

"Of course you don't," Arthur said, annoyed. "You just figured I would take care of it."

"You've tortured people before."

Arthur looked surprised, and a little hurt. Niccolo didn't much care right now. He had become too concerned with what *needed* to get done. They *needed* to do this. He'd never felt so sure of anything in his entire life.

"I've also turned my back on that person. The person I used to be has gone. He died when his family got butchered in their homes, or did you forget about that? I'm not a murderer anymore, and I don't torture people. I'm not that person."

Niccolo stared at Arthur for a moment. "Aren't you, though?"

"What?"

"You are the same person that stormed into that manor full of people and *murdered* them all."

"What I did—"

"That stain doesn't just *leave* you, Arthur. It doesn't just wash away when you change your clothes. You think that just because you feel guilty and want to imagine yourself as some sort of saint that you can become one? People don't change. I get that you feel bad for what you have done in the past, but that doesn't make you a different person."

Arthur didn't respond. It felt *good* to Niccolo to say this. To let it out finally. The truth was, no matter how hard Arthur tried to pretend that he had become a different person, he never would. He would always be a killer and ...

Something in his mind screamed that the situation felt wrong. He shook his head, replaying the conversation in his mind in horror. What had he just said? What had he *suggested*? He had thought of the idea of torture, but only for a second and had dismissed it easily.

So why had he suddenly grown so consumed with hatred and rage?

What was going on?

Those thoughts, like the others, got swept away.

"We can turn him over to the Church and let them deal with him," Arthur said, speaking slowly and studying Niccolo's face. He wore an expression of concern, now, like *he* thought something had gone wrong. "They will figure out what the bishop planned to do and save the children. But, I will not, under any circumstances, torture him for you."

"Because you're a coward," Niccolo said, almost in a snarl.

"Maybe you have it correct. But that doesn't mean —"

Niccolo felt another burst of rage. "You are a filthy-stinking-coward unwilling to do the necessary even when it stares you in the face."

Niccolo reached into the waistband under his coat, drew the gun he had tucked there, and aimed it at Arthur. The Hunter's eyes went wide, and he took a half-step backward. Niccolo savored the expression of shock when the man realized that Niccolo didn't hold one of his stupid tranquilizer guns.

No, this brought the real deal. Niccolo held a 9mm pistol, the one he had taken from the unconscious guard back at the water treatment plant and aimed at Garfield. He still had it with him, and it felt *good* in his hand.

What on Earth was going on?

Niccolo forced the thought away, focusing only on the euphoric rage pumping through his veins.

"This," he said, "has been a *long* time coming."

✳✳✳

Arthur realized something had happened to Niccolo, but he didn't know what. He wore a glazed look of anger on his face and didn't seem in control of himself.

But, if he had no control, then who did?

And why had Niccolo carried a real pistol with him?

"Why do you have ...?"

Niccolo held the gun steady. "You won't stand in my way, Arthur. Never again."

"What are you talking about?"

Suddenly, the front door to the office burst open, and two men came rushing into the room. Both armed with assault rifles, much like Naomi's soldiers at the water treatment plant earlier, and both had vacant expressions on their faces.

More demons.

As Arthur turned his head to get a good look at them, he noticed something else. Through the window of the office on the right-hand side, the face of a young boy, just barely a teenager, watched them. He had climbed onto the side of the trailer and peered in at them, staring directly at Niccolo with an expression of intense concentration on his face.

Arthur didn't know what was going on, but it couldn't be good.

"Uh oh."

He exploded into motion, reacting purely on instinct, and stepped in toward Niccolo. First, he pushed the priest's arm wide to force the barrel away from his body, and then used his free hand to punch him in the face.

He hit the priest hard and didn't hold back. Niccolo staggered under the weight of the blow. He hit the wall and dropped the gun, and Arthur rushed down and scooped it from the floor. This situation didn't leave room for his conscience. The time had come for action and survival.

Now armed, he turned to face the two masked intruders. They raised assault weapons and aimed at him, and he didn't have time to take aim and fire first.

Instead, he dove to the side through the connecting path of the two pre-fab structures. Just as they opened up with their rifles, he ducked behind the wall of that second mobile office.

A hail of bullets ripped through the area around him, and he crouched low while they shredded the material and sent dust and plaster flying. They tore through it like it wasn't even there. Arthur stayed low to the ground so that the bullets passed over his head.

He rolled to the side and crawled deeper into this second trailer, moving as quickly as he could while keeping his head down. The hut contained a table, a sofa, a television, two large metal cabinets, and little else.

He made his way over to the cabinets. Made of metal, hopefully they would prove thick enough to protect him from some of the rounds. Arthur rolled behind them, took a deep breath, and then checked the pistol Niccolo had brought. He must have stolen it from one of Naomi's mercenaries at the water treatment facility.

It looked cheap and had one full clip worth of ammo. The safety remained on—he doubted the priest had even known it had one—and looked as if it hadn't fired a shot in a long time. Arthur just had to hope it wouldn't jam.

Even with all of its problems, however, he still had to admit it felt good in his hand. Better than the light tranquilizer guns he'd carried. His instrument of choice, it felt like an extension of his existence.

No matter how far he ran from his true nature, he couldn't lie to himself. He had become good at killing people—a fact he hated about himself.

A few seconds passed, and then the hail of bullets died down. The demons would have to reload. Then they would come through the first trailer toward him. This offered his opportunity, and he didn't squander it.

He popped up over the cabinets. His guess proved correct. The first of his demonic pursuers just now stepped across the patched opening into the second trailer. A satisfying look of surprise settled on his face when he saw that Arthur didn't remain hidden where he had expected.

The expression lasted only a second before Arthur fired. He took careful aim, still unwilling to fire a kill-shot if he didn't have to. Instead, he shot the man in the left arm at the elbow and again on his right knee. Either wound would cripple the human whose body the demon rode. Without the body, the demon didn't pose much of a threat.

The man fell to the ground, and Arthur changed targets. The other demon had just finishing reloading his gun and now raised it, but he moved too slowly. Arthur fired, hitting him in the shoulder and again in each knee with three rapid shots.

This one dropped to the ground. Arthur had done significant damage to the hosts they lived in—if the men even continued to live—but with luck, they would survive.

Two down, but he hadn't freed himself from the woods yet. A second later, three more armed men came charging in through the doorway of the main trailer. He fired off two more shots, one hitting the first man in the stomach, and the second missing over his shoulder, and then the other two opened fire, forcing Arthur to duck.

These two didn't seem as dumb as the first pair. One fired while the other waited, and then they swapped while the first reloaded. The pistol Arthur carried only had a few rounds left in it, which wouldn't give him nearly enough to take down both men.

He looked around the room for something he could use as a distraction. The men closed in on him, and he was fast running out of time. He found nothing useful in range. The television had busted, riddled with holes, bullets had torn up most of the walls, and he hid behind the only real cover left in the room. Flimsy, it only managed to stop some of the bullets, forcing him to duck even lower than he would have liked.

Hopefully, Niccolo remained all right. Arthur had hit him harder than he probably needed to, and he hoped that either Niccolo wouldn't manage to get up and join the fray, or he would have smarts enough to stay down.

He had expected something to happen, but not quite with this level of force.

Also, Arthur realized that the bishop had played him. Everything he had said about his family had just given a distraction to keep him busy while Leopold's allies mounted a rescue. Arthur had allowed himself to get emotional and lose focus, and as such, they had now landed in a desperate situation they might not survive.

Unarmed and ill-prepared to deal with a threat of this magnitude, it meant trying to face-down two men armed with assault rifles with only a few rounds left in this pistol and his tranquilizer gun with its three shots—it would mean suicide.

He couldn't deal with them from in here. So, Arthur did the only thing he could—he shot out the nearest window and jumped into the shipyard.

✳✳✳

Arthur sprinted away from the office and through the empty shipyard, hoping to create as much distance as he could between him and his pursuers so that he could find some way out of this situation. He needed to turn the tide against them and force them to face him on even footing.

When he'd jumped through the window, he'd cut himself on his left arm with a glass shard, but the scrape didn't look too deep.

About halfway through the empty shipyard, movement came from behind him.

"Stop!"

The voice sounded commanding, though it came out high-pitched as if from a little kid. Arthur's legs locked, and he stopped running. All at once, he lost control of his body.

It felt intense and horrible, and he became powerless to keep moving forward. He looked back. The teenager who'd watched through the window stood next to the office and stared at him.

A thin and frail kid, his eyes glowed with an intensity and hate that filled Arthur with dread. Those eyes showed someone willing and able to kill if need be, and right now, they focused on Arthur.

The Hunter fought back, trying to reconcile his thoughts and regain control over his body. What a painstaking thing to do. Actions that would, normally, come as second-nature required actual thought. Mentally, he had to examine the process of walking and fire his muscles to get one of his legs to move.

He took a step forward.

"I said *stop*!"

Arthur focused on the other leg, and this time, it came a little easier. The other presences in his mind receded when he retook control. Another step, and then another, and gradually, he regained mastery over the motion. It felt like an hour passed during the struggle, but most likely only a few seconds had elapsed.

The presence remained in his mind, and his thoughts felt jumbled, but he managed to continue moving. He kept going, heading forward to the shipping containers.

✳✳✳

Niccolo's head spun, and his jaw hurt as he fumbled his way back to reality. The jaw he could explain because Arthur had punched him in the mouth and knocked him to the ground, but his head proved fuzzier and harder to understand.

It felt like all of his thoughts had jumbled together and distorted. He found it difficult to focus on anything in particular like someone had gone through and reorganized his mind. It felt … foreign.

Gunshots resounded in the room all around him. After a few seconds, though, they all went silent. People spoke, but he couldn't make out the words. Vaguely, he understood what had happened, and realized that they had come under attack, but he hadn't had any control.

What he had said to Arthur horrified the priest. Even

worse, they had all come from his deepest thoughts. He had buried them in his mind and would never have said them aloud, yet they had risen up and found release. It seemed as if his most basic of impulses had become unleashed, and he had become helpless to stop it.

The feeling of helplessness had disappeared now, but that didn't help him understand what had happened any better. When he managed to drag himself back to reality and look up, he saw the barrel of a rifle aimed at his face. A man stood above him, and beside him stood what looked like a teenage boy.

"He went out the window," a voice called out from the right. It took Niccolo a moment to recognize the voice as that of the bishop, and then his heart skipped a beat.

He meant Arthur. The Hunter had fled, leaving Niccolo behind.

"Should we go after him?"

"Yes! Nitwits. Go get him. But cut me loose first."

"What do we do with this one?" the other man asked, the one aiming his gun at Niccolo. He turned his head away from the priest and toward the bishop. "Want me to kill him?"

A second later and the first armed man had cut the bishop free. Glasser sat rubbing his wrists where the duct tape had bound him. Then he stood and walked over to where Niccolo slumped on the floor.

"No."

He looked down at Niccolo, a grin spreading across his face. A shiver ran up the priest's spine.

The bishop said, "Leave him to me."

Chapter 15

Arthur rushed over to the stacks of cargo containers running along the northern edge of the docks just as the bishop's men came out of the office to give chase.

The kid disappeared and had probably gone back into the building. His presence went from Arthur's mind, as well, but that didn't make the effect any less disorienting. The residual thoughts remained, making it hard for Arthur to think straight or focus on the task at hand.

His head ached, and he felt sick to his stomach from the recent invasion of his mind. That kid had crazy abilities, which also offered an explanation as to what had happened to Niccolo back in the trailer. No wonder Niccolo had lost it there for a while.

Arthur wracked his brain for a plan. The tranquilizer gun he had brought with him wouldn't prove effective against these demons, and the pistol he'd taken from Niccolo had run down to its last four bullets.

Arthur had no idea what had happened to Niccolo or if he even lived. The deck had stacked against them, and things looked grim.

And adding the kid to the mix made the tipping point. The child brought a wildcard that Arthur had not expected. Would never anticipate. He'd faced down a lot of crazy things in his time as a Hunter, but he had thought demons the worst creatures he would ever have to deal with. Some demons had innate power and proved dangerous, and occasionally, had telepathic or telekinetic abilities.

But those monsters Arthur had faced in his past paled in comparison to this Vatican Child working with the bishop. He had made Arthur feel like a ragdoll, completely unable to control his body.

If Arthur hadn't managed to break free of the kid's mental hold on him, then he would still have stood there, helpless, when the demonic mercenaries came outside to finish him off. The ease with which the kid had taken hold of his mind terrified Arthur.

He had to find some way to nullify the teenager's abilities if he planned to make it out of this alive.

The pursuers renewed fire, forcing Arthur to duck around the containers for cover. They remained a long way off, well out of range, but it still gave enough prompt to draw him out of his thoughts and back to the situation at hand. He wouldn't have the ability to do anything to stop the kid or get out of this situation while pinned down like this.

More gunshots thudded into the shipping containers and bounced off the metal. Some bullets created huge dents in the sides of the containers, and others ripped clear through the metal.

He ducked low to the ground and crawled away from the mercenaries, moving the short distance to the edge of this shipping container. Satisfied he remained out of their sight, he stood and ran toward another container about ten feet away. Then he slid behind it before his enemies could spot him and track his movements.

They would keep pursuing him into the lines of containers with the goal of flanking him. Arthur couldn't afford to stop moving and had to stay one step ahead of them to get the upper-hand. He could use their singular mission against them.

If only he had a plan or at least a distraction to give him the upper hand in this fight. He felt sorely unprepared for this and wished like hell for an extra clip of ammunition. Four shots meant that he couldn't afford to waste a single one, and still, they might not give him enough to take down both men.

He moved to the next container, ducking around the side to get a bead on the bishop's men. As expected, they had split apart and moved in parallel through the shipyard, trying to catch him in the middle.

They believed they had done themselves a favor and made it easier to catch the bishop. All they had done, in fact, was give him an edge.

***

Bishop Glasser reached down and dragged Niccolo to his feet. The priest struggled to fight back, but the bishop had considerably more strength than appearances indicated and lifted Niccolo with ease.

The fight had decimated the office around them. The wind whistled in through bullet holes, and the northern wall looked as though it might collapse at any moment.

A teenager stood grinning at him from the other side of the trailer, and two men lay on the ground with gunshot wounds, moaning in pain.

Given everything that had happened, it took him a moment to recognize the kid and remember where he had last seen him.

"Jeremy," he said on a heavy breath. No wonder the kid had sounded familiar. Niccolo had met him back in Everett.

"The one and only." The kid spread his arms and took a mocking bow.

Niccolo had met the boy at the bishop's estate when he'd first shown up in Everett. To think that the bishop had become so brazen as to keep the child with him even then, hiding him in plain sight. Niccolo had never even suspected.

"These two are losing control of their vessels," the kid said, speaking now to the bishop. He gestured toward the two men writhing on the ground. Arthur must have shot them. The wounds looked painful but not mortal.

"Then, help them maintain it. Get them back on their feet."

The kid fell silent for a moment, a thoughtful and intense look on his face. After a minute, he blinked and shook his head.

"I can't. The demons inside have grown too weak. The vessels have retaken control."

The bishop sighed, reached for his belt, and drew out a pistol. He walked over to one of the men who lay writhing on the ground. Wordlessly, he fired off two shots, putting each bullet into the man's head.

Then, he walked to the other side of the office and did the same to the other man. The gunfire echoed through the trailer, leaving behind only silence. Jeremy watched the bishop execute the men with a savage look on his face.

Finally, the bishop slid his gun away and turned to face Niccolo. He shrugged apologetically.

"It's so difficult to find good help."

"Maintain control," Niccolo said. "Jeremy gave you the ability to control the people of Everett, didn't he?"

The bishop looked pleased. "Yes, he did. It took just a few trips into town. He's like a nuclear bomb in demon possession. I did Rose personally, but the rest were Jeremy's pets. A few more weeks and I would have been able to wipe Everett off the map. How is that for waking the world?"

"You would kill all those people just to prove that demons exist?"

"Not kill," the bishop said. "They would become my army to let loose upon the world. Fanatics in a cause much bigger than themselves."

"They would have gotten slaughtered."

"The entire point. I expected someone like *you* to show up. Eventually, the Vatican would respond, and I would have had little trouble in getting you out of my way. I just didn't expect the Council to come to your aid so quickly. Not until after I had Haatim under my control, at least."

"Why do you want him?"

"I told you, he means *everything* to me. The things I could do with him and Jeremy together ... everything else just makes child's play."

"You call summoning and controlling demons child's play?"

"Trust me," the bishop said. "If you think me evil, you have *no* idea of what that child is capable. I could awaken Haatim's powers and turn him into a living weapon."

Niccolo didn't have a good response to that. He felt sick

and helpless in the situation, and they had vastly underestimated the bishop and his agenda. Though he had recognized that something terrible had happened in Everett, the scale of what the bishop had planned seemed much bigger than he could have imagined.

And seeing Jeremy, and what he could do ...

Terrifying.

"Now, you kill me?"

"Oh, no," the bishop said. "Kill you and waste such a valuable resource? Heavens, no."

"What, then?"

"I shall convert you."

***

"I'll *never* serve *you*."

"Not willingly," the bishop said. "But you *will* serve me. You'll make an excellent host."

"For what purpose?"

"I need an ally inside the Vatican. Someone who can report back to me on a regular basis about how the Church responds to my campaign."

"You intend to put one of your demons inside me?"

"Not just any demon," the bishop said. "Do you remember Rose? The demon inside her went by the name of Vasric. He's looked forward to having a more *personal* conversation with you ever since you exorcised him in Everett."

Niccolo went weak in the knees when the idea of becoming possessed washed over him. Just the mention of it horrified him. The priest would rather die than ever let one of those demons inside him.

"You can't win," Bishop Glasser said, watching his expression with satisfaction. "You can't stop me. The Church can't stop me. Arthur will die in only a few minutes, and you will become my slave. Or, maybe, I won't kill

Arthur. Maybe I will convert him as well. I could use an inside man in the Council, and he has quite the skill-set."

"Let me go after Arthur," Jeremy said. He stood in the doorway, looking out at the shipyard with a hungry expression. "I can bring him back in here with no trouble at all."

"You lost him once."

"He has more strength than I'd expected. I won't underestimate him again."

"No," the bishop said, patting Jeremy on the head. "You've done enough."

"But *you* said I could—"

Bishop Glasser flashed the kid a look, silencing him.

"I *know* what I said. You will get your chance soon enough, but right now, we need to get moving. We need to join your brothers and sisters aboard the ship. The time has not yet arrived to make your presence known."

Jeremy huffed but didn't object.

"Can I at least put the demon inside *him*?" He pointed at Niccolo.

Bishop Glasser glanced over at the priest. "Yes. Tonight. And then we will send him on his merry way back to the Vatican. Though not until I punish him for what he did to us. He cost me years of work when he dismissed Vasric in Everett."

More gunshots sounded in the distance as the mercenaries disappeared to the north. Niccolo prayed that Arthur remained alive and that they hadn't managed to trap him.

Arthur's unwillingness to kill had put them in this situation, and Niccolo's consternation and dislike of Arthur when first they met had inspired that attitude.

The irony of the situation proved twofold—Arthur's refusal to kill anyone would get them both killed, but, more importantly, Niccolo had learned that some people needed to die in order to end things.

Nothing good could come from letting a man like

Bishop Leopold Glasser live.

"Why do this?" Niccolo asked.

"Do what?"

"*This,*" Niccolo said, gesturing toward Jeremy. "These are children."

A look of anger flashed across the bishop's face. "Of *course* they are children, but that doesn't make them stupid, or useless. They have gifts and should receive respect."

"They should grow up as children, allowed to make decisions for themselves."

"As a society, we have trained ourselves to view children as weak and defenseless creatures, needing our protection and constant tutelage and capable of nothing valuable. We pretend they are ignorant to the ways of the world and need our guidance, but the truth is, they aren't the innocent little vessels we pretend. They are capable of *so* much more than we give them credit."

"It is our duty as a society to protect and nurture them."

"What do you think I've done? I've nurtured gifts you would rather pretend they don't have. I ask a lot of these children, true enough, and in return, they exceed my expectations. I ask you—why do some children grow up successful members of society while others fail? Because of *expectations.* I expect much from my children, and in return, they deliver beyond my wildest dreams."

"You know this is wrong," Niccolo said. "What you do goes against everything for which we stand."

"We?"

"The Church."

"Does it? Does my way truly go against what the Church stands for?"

"You conspire with demons and torture children."

"The demons serve me. They serve us, as they *should* always serve us. There was a time when the Church understood this."

"The demons kill people."

"*We* kill people. Does that make all humans evil, simply

because of the actions of a few?”

“I've never heard of demons doing good things.”

“That's because you've heard so little. The Church has indoctrinated you into believing demons embody evil and that special children bring an abomination that must get hidden away. The Church views us all as tools, little exorcists, and nothing else. The Church is at war with demon kind, and thus, they lash out. Could you expect anything else during wartime?”

“What utter nonsense.” Niccolo shook his head. “Nothing you say is true, and I can tell that even *you* don't believe the nonsense you espouse. This just makes a poor justification for what you do, because you *know* it is evil.”

Bishop Glasser shrugged. “I don't need to convince you. *You* are your own weakness, which is why you failed to stop me and will continue failing. I know you will not bring me to justice, no matter how evil you believe me to be, because you remain unwilling to do the necessary.”

Niccolo's hands trembled. “You are a monster.”

“One society's monster makes another society's hero. I shall wake the world and will not stop until everyone's eyes open. Even if you killed me—which you would never do— you still could not stop me. My ideas are bigger than my body and will continue on long after I die.”

The dread of the situation sank in on Niccolo, enveloping him like a blanket. A slow reality settled in and made him weak.

He should never have come here. He should never have believed that he could act as a soldier for God. He should never have thought that he could stop the bishop or put an end to any of this. Only a priest, an exorcist, Niccolo believed he made a poor one at that. This fell outside his world, and he had nothing to offer against an evil like this.

This world belonged to Arthur, dealing with threats that crossed the boundaries of human decency. For that reason, the Church had and needed such soldiers at their disposal. It gave the raison d'être for the Council of Chaldea and other such organizations—to do the unspeakable things required to keep the world safe.

Until this moment, Niccolo had never truly believed them necessary, and now he understood that, sometimes, no other recourse remained. Occasionally, the only way to stop evil was with evil.

He had done harm to Arthur's identity and contributed to the guilt that put him in this weakened position. The priest held no illusions that he held partial—maybe most—blame for Arthur's newfound inability to kill, and as such, Arthur had to face-off against two heavily-armed men with only a tranquilizer gun with which to defend himself.

Niccolo had never felt so helpless or *wrong* in his entire life. They would both die here in this shipyard because of decisions Niccolo had made. The bishop would walk free and continue his crusade against the world, and Niccolo could do nothing about it.

✳✳✳

Arthur had nearly run out of places to hide. He'd managed to stay one step ahead of his pursuers, but they now tightened the noose around his neck, and it wouldn't take long before they got a clear shot on him.

The two men pursuing him took an incredibly methodical approach, working as a team to make sure that neither of them ever became over-exposed. He had hoped to isolate one of them and take him down, but they made that difficult.

Several times, he might have managed to get a clean shot at one of them, and maybe even drop one, but it would expose him to a clear shot from the other guy. He couldn't take the risk of letting one of them get a few shots with the assault rifle. In that case, he wouldn't be asking for luck—it would be suicide.

Not only did Arthur need to isolate one of them, but also to close the distance. How could he get close to one of them, though, without getting seen?

He slid his tranquilizer gun away and scanned the area around him. His best option, he realized, lay in going up on top of the containers.

Made of metal, they would make his climb loud, though, and in the silent shipping yard, any sound echoed. If he tried to climb atop one, and they knew so, then he would, basically, have turned himself into a fish in a barrel.

Luckily, even though it had stopped raining, it remained fairly windy. If he timed his movements perfectly, he could get on top without the noise carrying.

The problem with that, though, lay in that he didn't have a lot of time to climb slowly and time his movements, and he didn't want to get caught on the side of the container.

He had to risk it, though. Otherwise, eventually, the mercenaries would catch up to him.

Jaw tight, he climbed the side of one of the containers, moving slowly and carefully so as not to make any extra noise. The containers stood about ten-feet tall and stacked one on top of another two rows high. If the guard rounded the corner behind him while he climbed, he would become a sitting duck, but he still couldn't risk going too fast.

Luck stayed with him, and the overly cautious actions of his pursuers played to his advantage. He slipped over to the top of the shipping container, rolling flat onto his stomach and into the shadows only a few seconds before one of the masked men rounded the corner behind him.

Prone, he steadied his breathing and ducked his head out of sight, focusing entirely on listening to the world around him for the man's approach.

The guy moved fairly quietly, but Arthur could still hear him coming from down below. Also, though faintly, Arthur heard his friend another row over, moving steadily toward a crossing point where they would converge once more. They wanted to flush him out, and it grew clear they didn't know he had gone up above.

Arthur would only have a few seconds of advantage

once he gave away his position before the other man rounded the corner and had a clear view of him, so he would need to make sure those seconds counted.

He waited until the masked man reached only a few steps in front of and below his hiding spot before sliding forward. The man tensed, hearing Arthur move, but too late. He swung his weapon up toward Arthur but too slow.

Arthur dropped from the top of the stack of containers onto the mercenary, kicking him hard on his shoulders and knocking him sideways.

The man staggered into the shipping container, and Arthur landed on the ground. He hit the pavement a lot harder than he would have liked, but the attack partly broke his fall. The jolt ran up his legs, and he let out a grunt of pain, but he had to ignore it for now.

He rushed forward before the demon could recover, punching the man in the throat and shoving the tip of his assault rifle away so that it aimed away from his body.

The man pulled the trigger anyway, attempting to swing it back toward Arthur. The air filled with the sudden thunder of multiple gunshots firing into the air. Arthur held the barrel of the weapon away from his body and lashed out again, punching the man hard in the chest this time.

The mercenary staggered back, trying to create separation between him and Arthur to use his rifle, but the Hunter didn't give him the chance.

Instead, he stepped in closer, kicked the man in the ankle, and then yanked the barrel of the gun forward. He couldn't take the gun from the man—he had it clipped to his vest—but that wasn't the point anyway.

Able to use the momentum of the jerking motion, Arthur dragged the guy forward and off-balance. He glanced to the side. The second guard rounded the corner and came in at him.

This demon didn't seem too concerned about his friend's safety. He raised the gun up as soon as Arthur came in sight and fired at them both.

Arthur reacted quickly and dragged the staggered man in between him and the shooter, using the man as a body shield. He wore Kevlar, but the heavy rounds ripped right through the first layer as if no more than a t-shirt.

They weren't quite strong enough to make it out the back side of the armor, though, and Arthur could feel them ripping around inside the man's body as they bounced off the armored plates.

He could only imagine the pain and devastation those bullets did inside the man's chest cavity. He tried not to think about it too hard.

The other attacker kept firing, and the brunt of the bullets pushed him backward and down. He stayed low, waiting until the clip ran empty and the man had to reload.

Then Arthur shoved the limp body forward, drew the pistol he'd taken from Niccolo, and fired off all four shots. He aimed for the man's kneecaps, crippling the body with the first two shots, and then the last two, he put into the left shoulder so that the guy couldn't fire the gun.

The man collapsed to the ground and screamed in agony, clutching his knees and writhing in pain.

The screams sounded genuine, but Arthur couldn't tell for sure. He drew his tranquilizer gun and approached cautiously. Was this some trap?

The guy thrashed and screamed, and when he saw Arthur, he groaned in pain and crawled toward him.

"Please," he said. "Please, help me. What's going on? Please, you have to help me!"

"Has it gone?"

"Has what gone?"

Arthur had an easy way to find out. He aimed in and fired off the tranquilizer dart, hitting the man right in his exposed neck. The man fell limp almost at once, completely unconscious.

"Guess he told the truth."

Arthur rushed forward, grabbed the bottom of the man's shirt, and ripped off a piece to use as a tourniquet.

Four shots had been a lot, but he felt confident they wouldn't kill him outright. If he bled out, though, that would be another story. Arthur would need to get the guy to help quickly to have any chance of saving his life.

✳✳✳

The shooting stopped outside, and a heavy silence descended over the office. The bishop stood still in the center of the trailer, listening, and then turned to face Niccolo with a smile.

"Looks like Arthur is no more," he said. "A pity. I would have loved to use him for my own purposes, but he remained too dangerous to—"

"I don't sense them," Jeremy said, still staring outside the front door of the building. He turned to face the bishop, a horrified look on his face. "I don't sense them anymore."

The bishop frowned. "What do you mean?"

Without responding, Jeremy turned and ran out of the building and toward the shipping containers. He rushed down the ramp and out of sight.

"Wait!" the bishop shouted, moving to follow him.

Niccolo seized the distraction on an impulse, rushing forward and grabbing the bishop around the waist. He tried to tackle the man to the floor, but again, he found out that the bishop had considerably more strength than he appeared to have.

Leopold Glasser turned and shoved Niccolo against the wall, slamming him hard against the wooden interior wall of the building. Niccolo shoved back, pushing Leopold off him and trying to kick him.

They punched and scrapped, each trying to get the upper hand. Finally, the priest managed to tackle the bishop around the waist successfully. Niccolo lifted the bishop and threw him to the ground, and in the motion, the gun in the bishop's waistband popped out and went skidding across the floor.

The bishop punched him in the jaw and tried to jerk loose, crawling toward the gun. Niccolo refused to let go, dragging Leopold away in the opposite direction and climbing to his feet.

The bishop stood as well, launching a flurry of punches at Niccolo to force him backward. Niccolo did his best to hold his own, giving ground, and then he kicked the bishop again in the knee. This time, the bishop hit *him* low, aiming for his knees and knocking him over.

They both hit the ground, and then Niccolo rolled over top and past the bishop, climbing to his feet and rushing forward to where the gun lay on the floor of the trailer. The bishop came right on his heels, but Niccolo managed to get hold of the grip of the gun, spin, and raise it into the bishop's face.

Leopold stopped midstride, the gun only inches from his nose. He had a bloody lip and a cut on his forehead, but otherwise, he looked all right. In submission, he held up his hands, taking a step back.

"All right," he said. "You win."

"On your knees," Niccolo said. "Put your hands behind your head."

The bishop stood there for a long second, an ugly smile spreading across his face. Slowly, he lowered his hands to his sides.

"I said, on your knees!"

"You won't shoot me. That would be murder, and *cold-blooded* murder at that. You would never stoop so low."

"I'll do it," Niccolo said, his voice higher pitched than he would have liked. He didn't sound that convincing. "Don't make me shoot you."

"You can't, though. You can't do it. Even after all of this, even after all of the things I've done, and the things I will do, you still *can't* kill me."

"Last chance," Niccolo said. "Get on the ground."

"Or what?" the bishop asked.

Suddenly, Leopold stepped forward, reaching out for

the gun to try and grab it from Niccolo. The priest didn't think, only reacted.

He pulled the trigger.

Epilogue

Arthur still tended to the man he had shot when a gunshot came from the direction of the office building. Hopefully, it wasn't Niccolo hit. He needed to get back there and find out what had happened.

Movement came from behind him. He spun, raising his tranquilizer gun. The teenager stood maybe forty meters away.

However, the kid didn't stand looking at him. He stared back the way he had come, at the office trailers. Then, slowly, he turned to face Arthur.

His young face held a terrified expression, but with hatred mixed in. A look that Arthur had never experienced before. Neither of them moved for what felt like minutes.

Arthur prepared himself for whatever the kid might throw at him. He still had two darts in the tranquilizer gun to use on him and figured if he could get a single shot at a closer range, he could take down the boy. After all, the teenager remained only human, so the darts would work on him for definite.

Just about to move forward, Arthur stopped dead. All of a sudden, the boy had gone. Disappeared. One second, he stood there in front of him, and the next, Arthur just gaped down an empty corridor at nothing.

It had a disjointing effect on him like his eyes had played tricks on him, but he knew it was real. Arthur stood, walked over to where the kid had stood and stared at him, but found nothing.

"What the hell?"

He hurried back to the office. It felt as if he'd lost time, and that maybe a few minutes had passed without his knowledge. When he got inside, he found Niccolo sitting in the center of the trailer with a blank expression on his face.

On the floor in front of him lay what was left of the bishop.

Shot in the left eye, a gaping hole ran clear through his

head. The man lay utterly dead. The other two men that Arthur had wounded had also died, shot in the head from close range, but he didn't believe that Niccolo had done that.

He hoped, at least.

Niccolo just sat there, staring at the body in disbelief. He still held the weapon he'd used to kill the bishop, and blood had splattered his face and clothes. As he looked up at Arthur, the priest's hands trembled.

"I warned him ..."

Arthur couldn't think of anything useful to say. Sirens wailed in the distance, heading their way. They only had a couple of minutes to get out of there before the place would swarm with police.

"We need to go."

Niccolo looked up at him blankly. "What?"

"We need to get out of here. Cops are on their way."

"Oh," Niccolo said. "All right."

He rose mechanically, walked past Arthur, and out of the front doorway of the office. He barely seemed to have a grasp of what happened and looked like a thoroughly confused man.

Everything had gone wrong.

Arthur took one more look at the dead bishop and then followed Niccolo out to the car. Arthur hated to leave the wounded men like this, but he had to trust that the paramedics would save at least the one man's life.

They saw no sign of the kid on the docks, and everything seemed quiet. They climbed into the car and sped away from the shipyard.

✳✳✳

Arthur spoke with Frieda as they drove away from the docks, explaining everything that had gone down in the last couple of days and that the bishop had died. She'd spoken to Garfield already—who felt pissed at him—and she didn't sound too happy with the way things had gone. Especially with the murder of the bishop, and it shocked her when he said that Niccolo had pulled the trigger.

She did manage to find a nearby hotel where they could lay low, and Arthur got Niccolo inside as fast as he could so that they could get cleaned up. Niccolo didn't speak and had withdrawn into himself, but he did respond to what Arthur said. The Hunter managed to get them both cleaned up and hid their bloody clothes.

Then, with no other recourse except to wait it out and hear back from Frieda, Arthur went to sleep. Exhausted and running on fumes, he saw no sense in worrying about things he couldn't change.

When he awoke the next morning, he found Niccolo in the chair in the corner of their hotel room—the same place he'd sat when Arthur had fallen asleep. He doubted he'd moved the entire night, and he still had that vacant expression on his face.

Arthur let him be, and instead, called Frieda to get an update. She informed him that police had swarmed the shipyard during the night and had located six children on the boat, in one of the crew's quarters.

They had also identified the dead bishop and a number of other deceased men. One wounded man remained in critical condition and might or might not pull through.

The Hunter asked Frieda to pass on the information about the attacks throughout the country, and then he hung up. He doubted he would hear from her again for a while until she had more news to report.

The next two days, he spent in the hotel room or out getting food while they waited for updates. Niccolo barely spoke the entire time, accepting offered food, using the facilities, and just sitting in the chair.

Finally, Frieda called them to fill them in on events. The Church had collected the children and needed to process, and it also wanted a full reporting from Niccolo about what had happened and why he had gone so far outside his jurisdiction without their permission.

"What about the bishop?" Arthur asked.

"It didn't please them that you killed him," she said, "but they've covered it up. It turns out that a lot of evidence on the boat backed up your story and solidified what happened in Everett. They realize that things had to move quickly and don't feel mad at you. All in all, things turned out a lot better than they might have."

"That's good."

"Not really. It's started already. A child in Idaho killed five people this morning, and folks claim that something suspicious happened. It won't take long until the Church can't contain this. They've asked me to pull every Hunter onto this case."

"It isn't over," Arthur said. "I need to get to Ohio. That's where one of the strongest went. Something will happen there."

"I know," Frieda said. "You need to get on the road and stop them."

"What about Niccolo?"

"I don't know," she said. "The Church plans on having a long conversation with him, but for now, they just want all of this to get dealt with."

"All right. I'll call you when I get on the road. I should reach Ohio in a couple of days."

"Arthur," Frieda said before he could hang up. "I know you don't want to hear this, but ... when you get to Ohio, you should go home."

He fell silent for a long moment. Finally, he sighed. "You're right," he said. "I don't want to hear that."

Then he hung up. He sat there for a long while, just letting the silence hang over the hotel room, before he finally walked over to where Niccolo sat.

"We need to keep moving," he said. "This hasn't finished. At least two kids remain missing. We need to stop them before they can enact whatever plan the bishop left for them."

"I should turn myself over to the Church," Niccolo said in a flat voice. "So they can excommunicate me."

"Yes," Arthur said. "You should. Just not yet."

"Why?"

"Because I need your help."

Niccolo laughed sardonically. "Help? Help with what? I've only managed to make things worse and slow you down."

"What you did back there—"

"What I did was murder," Niccolo said with vehemence. "Plain and simple. No two ways about it. I killed a man in cold-blood."

"You didn't have a choice."

"We always have a choice."

"Nevertheless," Arthur said. "I need your help to stop the things happening. People have died already. If you feel you deserve punishment, then accept your chastisement, but right now, we need to halt this threat before more people get hurt."

Niccolo hesitated before turning to look at Arthur. "Fine," he said with a look of immense pain in his eyes. "I'll help. And then I'll turn myself in."

Arthur nodded. "Good."

"What about Haatim?"

Arthur froze. "What about him?"

"He's one of the children. He's on the list Naomi gave you, isn't he?"

Arthur didn't want to voice his concern aloud about that list because he felt afraid of the information making it back to the Vatican. He didn't know if the Church knew about Haatim or not, but if they didn't, then he had no intention to bring it up. Especially not after what the bishop had said.

He decided, though, to trust Niccolo. "Haatim is a child of one of the Council members. I rescued him back in Everett, but I didn't know any of *this* at that point in time."

"We should warn the Church."

"We shouldn't," Arthur said. "The bishop has died. Naomi has gone on the run. The threat to Haatim and the other children on the list is over with."

"He remains one of the Vatican Children. The Church should know about them."

"Let me ask you honestly," Arthur said. "Should a list exist at all?"

Niccolo stayed silent.

"If you want my honest opinion about this, then we should just forget about the list. I'll destroy it and have it done with. With the bishop dead, I reckon these children have suffered through enough."

"You ask me to forget about what the bishop said?"

"I ask you not to tell the Church about it," Arthur said. "Haatim is just a kid, and he doesn't deserve to go through something like what these children had to experience. No one does. The Church tracking special children and trusting Bishop Glasser caused this entire situation, and maybe it is better if we just forget about it."

Niccolo thought about it. "Okay," he said. "I won't tell the Church."

"Thank you."

"What now?"

"Now," Arthur said, turning back to pack his bags. "We head to Ohio."

About the Author

Lincoln Cole is a Columbus-based author who enjoys traveling and has visited many different parts of the world, including Australia and Cambodia, but always returns home to his pugamonster, Luther, and wife. His love for writing was kindled at an early age through the works of Isaac Asimov and Stephen King, and he enjoys telling stories to anyone who will listen.